The Mystery of The Pink Aura

A Witch's Cove Mystery
Book 3

Vella Day

The Mystery of The Pink Aura
Copyright © 2020 by Vella Day
Print Edition
www.velladay.com
velladayauthor@gmail.com

Cover Art by Jaycee DeLorenzo
Edited by Rebecca Cartee and Carol Adcock-Bezzo

Published in the United States of America
Print book ISBN: 978-1-951430-09-2

A psychic vision. Missing contestants. A witch and her pink iguana sidekick.

Witch's Cove, the idyllic Florida beach town, is finally getting their long-awaited deputy. The problem is that no one can dig up anything on him—good or bad—and that sets off alarms for the gossip queens.

Hi, I'm Glinda Goodall, the amateur sleuth who works at the Tiki Hut Grill. The sheriff works hard and deserves good help, but is the new deputy, Nash Solano, really who he says he is? The day after he arrives, chaos descends on the town— as in, two contestants in a regional dog show go missing shortly after a psychic sees a mysterious pink aura around them.

The sheriff has been good to me and my talking pink iguana. So naturally, I have to investigate—both the deputy and the missing competitors. As is always the case, things never go as planned.

If you want to learn more, stop by the Tiki Hut Grill and give Iggy and me a hand in solving this crazy mystery.

Chapter One

If this is the first book in the series for you, or you need a refresher, check out my website for who is who (scroll down).

velladay.com/mysteries.html

PENNY CARSTED, MY coworker and best friend, rushed up to me and tugged on my sleeve, clearly needing my attention. "Glinda, did you hear?"

I set the full sugar shaker down on the side table in the Tiki Hut Grill where we both waitressed and faced her. Despite her out loud squeal, my heart didn't race, because I knew everything was a big deal to Penny. It was one of the many reasons why I adored her. "Hear what?"

"We have a new deputy!"

Okay, I hadn't expected that announcement, and I will admit my pulse actually jumped. "It's about time. What do we know about him?" I asked, letting my never-ending curiosity get the best of me.

I assumed the new addition to the sheriff's department was male, because the Witch's Cove city council was responsible for hiring this person. And, well, let's say our beloved rulers were basically a good old boys club.

Why did I care? I had recently *unofficially* worked with

Sheriff Steve Rocker on a case that involved the murdered nephew of one of our very own, and I wanted to make sure the city council hired someone who would be an asset. At least, that was what I told myself.

Why did I assume Penny would know about our new deputy? Easy. Even on the day of his arrival, the whole town would have learned if he was married—did or did not have kids—what his favorite foods were, and what his shirt size was. The last statistic might seem strange to the average person, but the five gossip queens of Witch's Cove were all single, and it wouldn't be unkind of me to say that four of the five had a roaming eye. It wasn't just me who thought that. All of them would readily admit it too, especially Dolly Andrews, the owner of the Spellbound Grill.

My sixty-three-year-old Aunt Fern was the exception. She claimed she wasn't looking for a man, but I think if the right person came along, she might change her mind. While I now had the ability to see her husband's ghost, I think Uncle Harold would want her to be happy too.

"What do I know?" Penny asked, finally answering me. "Nothing, nada, zilch, and that is the problem. What is happening to this town?"

I chuckled to cover up my embarrassment that I hadn't heard even that much. "You have no information other than he's arrived?"

"No, and to make matters worse, I ran into Dolly, and she only knew that he came into town late last night. Apparently, there are no stats on him—including what his name is."

Wow. That was a first. Clearly, these women were slacking. "Let's ask Aunt Fern," I suggested. A person couldn't sneeze in town without everyone learning about it—in part because my nosy aunt had a direct line to the sheriff's grandmother, Pearl Dillsmith, who happened to be the receptionist at the sheriff's department. I figured that intel was as good as anyone could get. Pearl would have met this newcomer and hopefully would have told her friends all about him already.

If the information flow was ever slow in coming from her gossipy friends, my aunt, who owned the Tiki Hut Grill, would hear about it from someone in her restaurant.

At the moment, she was working the checkout counter. Since she wasn't helping anyone, both Penny and I went up to her.

"Hey, Aunt Fern." Needing to make a bit of small talk first to grease the wheel so to speak, I peeked over the counter to see if her newly adopted cat, Aimee, was keeping her company. She was not, and that concerned me a bit. "Is Aimee with Iggy?"

Iggy was my familiar—a very chatty pink iguana—who considered himself a sleuth. As ridiculous as that might sound, he did have a knack for finding useful information.

"I doubt it. I think they had another fight."

"I hadn't heard about it." Why was I being left out of everything? My heart ached for my poor familiar. Iggy really liked Aimee. Even though this new arrival had only recently been given the magical power of speech, she was still a cat— one who gave affection only when she saw fit. "What can you tell me about the new deputy?" I asked.

My aunt's eyes suddenly brightened. It was because she loved being the disseminator of gossip. "According to Pearl, he is quite the looker. Dark haired, olive skinned, and he has the bluest eyes she's even seen."

Considering Pearl was in her late seventies, I'm not so sure I could trust her description. "Apart from his dashing good looks, what do we know about him?"

"He's from Montana."

That was a far cry from Florida. "Then I don't blame him for wanting a change of scenery." That wasn't quite the information I was looking for, but it was better than nothing.

"What else, Fern?" Penny asked. "Does this handsome stranger have a name?"

A blank look crossed her face. "You know, I don't think Pearl mentioned it. I think the sheriff came in when she was giving me the deets, but don't you worry, I'll find out what I can and let you two know."

Penny smiled. "Thanks."

I motioned to Penny that we get out of the way of the customer who had just walked up with his bill and credit card in hand.

"Did you teach her to say *deets*?" I whispered as I guided us back to the condiment table.

"Yes. If she's ever going to attract a man, she needs to sound hip."

I barked out a short laugh. "My aunt isn't looking to date."

Penny waved a hand. "Everyone is looking."

There was no use arguing with her. We had been friends for three years, and once Penny made up her mind, there was no changing it. I might have pressed the issue, but I had the feeling my aunt enjoyed the hip-speak lessons.

Just as I was about to speculate on this new Montana cowboy, the front doors flew open, and I swear a whole busload of people rushed in. My aunt thanked the customer at the counter and then hustled over to the newcomers to find tables for all of them. She didn't need to tell us it was time to move into action. We knew the drill.

As I spun around to get back to work, my pink tiara shifted on my head and nearly fell off. Why was I wearing cheap plastic headgear? Simple. All employees were required to wear a costume. Aunt Fern had believed it would help draw in the tourists, and she had been right. Without a doubt, business had picked up ever since we had started dressing up for work.

Why a pink tiara, you might ask? My mother was a *Wizard of Oz* fanatic, which was why she named me Glinda. It made sense too since I am a witch—albeit not a great one— and we live in the south. Even though I was teased a lot growing up for having that name, I eventually grew to like it, mostly because the movie witch always wore pink—my favorite color.

"Glinda!" my aunt called. "Tables one, four, and seven are waiting."

Daydreaming was my worst flaw—or rather one of my worst. "On my way."

I loved being a waitress, but only when I had the time to chat with the customers. Today, however, would not give me that rush since there wouldn't be time to make any sort of connection. I strode over to table one. I'd never seen this couple before, so I suspected they were tourists.

"Hey, there. I'm Glinda. Are you here for our sandy

beaches and brilliant sunshine?" I asked with practiced perfection.

"Not this time. We might take a dip in the Gulf, but we came for the dog show."

How could I have forgotten about that big event? It was the first annual agility dog training competition in Witch's Cove. "Are you showing a dog?"

She chuckled. "Oh, no. We have a mutt who rarely follows directions, unless it's time to eat or go for a walk. But we love him to death." The woman, who was in her mid-forties, had bright purple hair streaked with pretty blue and green highlights. "I wish we could afford one of those agility dogs, but those pooches are too expensive for our blood."

"I hear ya." About not being able to afford a show dog, that is. I could never have a dog. Iggy would tease the poor pup to death. Not only that, my familiar wasn't big on competing for my affection. "I look forward to checking out the show after work. It should be fun. What can I get you?" I couldn't afford to dawdle today.

After they ordered, I headed over to my next table. This was a family of four who were also here for the dog show, but these were competitors. "Our dog won in Delmar, so he's ready to compete in this Master Class competition," the mother said.

"That's amazing." I'd heard that the original site for the show had to cancel for some reason, though I had no idea this show was at that level. "What kind of dog is he?"

"Snookums is a Papillon."

Snookums? I shouldn't be one to judge. Maybe it was why I gave Iggy a boring name—or so he reminded me all of the time. I didn't want to admit I'd never heard of that breed. "I wish you luck."

"Thanks."

I really needed to find out more about this event. I'd been so busy trying to solve the mystery of who killed Morgan Oliver last month, that I hadn't kept up on current events. I had heard that Eleanor Aldrich was in charge of this dog event and that it was supposed to bring in a lot of revenue to the town. I just never took the time to find out the details. I'd have to ask Iggy tonight what he knew. Between him and his no-longer girlfriend—the talking cat—they might know.

"What can I get you?" I asked.

After poring over the menu, they finally ordered. Before I took the order at my third table, I dropped the first two requests off at the kitchen. While I was happy for Aunt Fern and her bottom line, having only Penny with me to handle all ten inside tables was hectic at best. I was sure the two outside patio servers had it just as bad though.

As I approached table seven, I glanced over at Penny, who seemed more stressed than I was. She was already a bit high-strung, probably because she had to raise a seven-year-old mostly by herself. Her ex-husband did help by taking and picking up Tommy at school.

The forty-five to fifty-year-old gentleman at my table was wearing a pair of navy blue slacks and a well-pressed white shirt with gold cuff-links. I couldn't remember the last time I'd seen this kind of attire during the hot summer months—especially in here. His nails were polished and his eyebrows manscaped. Most people probably didn't notice those kind of details, but wild hair randomly jutting above a person's eyes disturbed me.

Since the man had placed the many-paged menu on the table and looked up, I figured he was ready.

"Hi there, I'm Glinda, what can I get you?" He didn't look like the type who desired a conversation.

"A coffee with a quarter teaspoon of cinnamon and a dollop of cream—but don't overdo it. And some real sugar, please. I don't use that *fake* stuff." He tugged on his long sleeves, probably to show off that he had money. "I'll have the baked fish. Please ask the chef not to dry it out."

He was a piece of work, but I'd met worse. "Sure thing. Are you here for the dog show?" I'd learned that this influx of folks all seemed to have come for that.

"Yes. My Mittens is one of the contestants. He's a Border Collie. Keep an eye on him. He's a winner." I couldn't decide if he actually smiled or if he had gas.

"I can't wait." Or not.

There was something off-putting about this man, but why should it matter? I'd promised myself that I was finished with sticking my nose in where it didn't belong.

As I scurried to the kitchen to drop off his request, my aunt motioned me over. "Yes?"

"Table six needs more coffee, and table nine says the food is cold," my aunt said, sounding as stressed as I felt.

"I'll take care of it." I waved the orders to show her I wasn't slacking.

I started working here three years ago, right after I decided that being a middle school math teacher wasn't for me. During that time, I don't remember it ever being this packed, especially in the middle of July when it rained pretty much every day.

Someone should have warned us that this many people would descend for this dog show. Who knew they were so popular?

For the next hour and a half until my shift ended, it was non-stop work. Not that I didn't appreciate the tips, but I couldn't chat with anyone since I was either taking orders or running food to the tables.

By the time the next set of servers showed up, I was tired, but not too tired to check out the new deputy.

It wasn't so much that I liked to snoop—or had an inner drive to meddle—but it was that I cared about our sheriff and wanted to make sure he was getting the help he deserved. Steve Rocker had only arrived in town seven weeks ago, but I'd quickly figured out he was one of the good guys. With the addition of this new deputy, Witch's Cove now had two newcomers.

I smiled. Steve Rocker had come a long way since his arrival. At first, he'd been skeptical about my ability to determine the cause of death by waving a pink crystal over the deceased's body, but eventually he stopped thinking of me as some crazy lady who considered herself a witch. Now, I think he sees me as a necessary evil.

After refilling the salt and pepper shakers once more, I clocked out. Since I lived in one of the two apartments above the restaurant, I ran upstairs to my place. Iggy, my familiar, was on his usual rattan stool looking out at the beach and the slightly overcast sky.

"A lot of people here for the dog show?" he asked without turning around. "It sounded loud downstairs."

I lifted off my crown. "You have no idea." I explained about the dog show. "From what I gathered, it's two days of agility training and then the show itself. Good thing I have tomorrow off so I can check it out." Penny had asked if I'd work Sunday for her. In exchange, she'd work tomorrow for me. It was a win-win solution. "I'm too old to be working three days straight in this madhouse."

Twenty-six might seem young to most, but after learning I could suddenly see ghosts, I hadn't slept well. I needed a break.

After entering my bedroom, I changed out of my witch costume. I then pulled on a pair of dark pink shorts, a sleeveless rose top, and my pink sandals. If I didn't make it clear before, I like pink. In fact, I only wear pink.

After checking my wardrobe choice in the mirror to make sure I looked presentable, I returned to the living room. And no, I wasn't thinking about impressing our hot newcomer by putting on one of my better outfits.

Iggy turned around and hopped down from his stool. "Don't we look pretty."

I doubted it was a compliment. "I just changed into shorts."

"Uh-huh. I bet you're going to check out the new deputy, aren't you?" he asked in a teasingly sing-song voice.

How did everyone know about him but me? "What do you know?"

"Do you have any arugula leaves? I'm hungry."

Answer avoidance was a sure sign he was trying to exchange information for food. "I have to bribe you for information now? I thought we were partners."

Iggy had the decency to look away. A few seconds later, he looked back at me—or rather his eyes that were located on the side of his head faced me. I knew how to out stare him though.

"I would tell you more, but I don't know much. I'm waiting to see what everyone else learns," he said.

"Fine. I'll fix you some leaves, but next time, please be honest with me."

After I set out something for him to eat, I grabbed my keys and phone, ready to head out on my fact-finding mission. Once downstairs, I asked Aunt Fern for a ten-dollar gift certificate. I thought it would be fun to be the welcoming committee of one.

Chapter Two

WITH MY GIFT card in hand, I headed across the street to the sheriff's department, surprised at the number of people out and about. Were they all here to watch the agility competition? I couldn't think of another explanation. At some point, I planned to go to the park and see what it was all about.

Other than to welcome the deputy to Witch's Cove, and mentally record my first impression, I wasn't sure what I would say to him. Asking too many questions would raise a flag since he'd surely wonder why I was so curious.

Regardless of what I asked, the deputy would probably think I was weird. Being a good detective, he'd ask Pearl or the sheriff about me. In either case, I hope they'd both say I was merely eccentric. If I was really lucky, Steve would admit that I had helped solve two recent crimes. (To be honest, without my help, I'm not sure if he would have figured out either case.)

I inhaled to fortify my courage and then pushed open the door, expecting to see Pearl either knitting at her desk, chatting on the phone, or flipping through some pages in an attempt to look busy. Instead, Jennifer Larson was at the reception desk. Darn. I really needed to memorize Pearl's schedule.

I liked Jennifer, a young mother of two, but it was just that if she knew any gossip, she wasn't the sharing type. As unobtrusively as possible, I looked around for the new guy but didn't see him—or the sheriff for that matter.

"Hey, Jennifer. Where is everyone?" I didn't want to ask for the deputy specifically.

She smiled. "Both Nash and Steve are at the park."

Nash? That was an interesting name. "They're into dogs?"

She chuckled. "No, they are there for crowd control."

"I haven't been to the event yet, but the streets sure are crowded. I had no idea so many would show up."

"The organizer told Steve to expect over a thousand people."

I whistled. The town of Witch's Cove only had about two thousand inhabitants. "Good to know. It's no wonder the Tiki Hut was swamped today."

"I imagine it will be that way for the next few days. Ted told me that the Magic Wand Hotel had been booked for this event for weeks."

His hotel would only hold a fraction of the newcomers. "Where are the rest staying?" We only had a few smaller motels on the edge of town.

"That I couldn't say."

I probably wouldn't learn anything by sticking around, so it was best to leave. "Thanks for the info."

Next, I headed out to the park, which sat at the end of the main row of establishments. It wasn't a large piece of land. A thousand visitors would put a strain not only on the parking, but on the bathrooms as well. I imagined all restaurants and shops would get a lot of traffic, too, asking to use their facilities. Most wouldn't mind, but like all towns, we had our share of curmudgeons.

As I approached the area where people congregated, my right sandal sunk into the slightly muddy grass. Ugh. It had rained last night, and the sun had yet to dry out every nook and cranny. I never should have worn my good shoes, but I wasn't going to let that stop me from meeting the new guy in town. As I scoped out the area, my chances of even seeing the dogs appeared to be slim. Witch's Cove should have built bleachers or something.

While crowded, finding Steve Rocker wasn't hard. At six-feet four, the guy was a bear of a man, and as such, easy to spot. Both he and another man, who was about thirty-five, were standing off to the side. Given the man's matching uniform, I concluded he must be Nash from Montana.

With my excuse in hand, I walked up to them. "Sheriff, nice day for a dog show."

His pretty eyes shone. "It is, but I thought you were more of the exotic pet type of person."

Iggy would like the exotic part of the comment, but not the pet part. "I am." Before Steve could tell me both he and Nash were busy, I turned to the newcomer. "Hi, I'm Glinda Goodall. My aunt owns the Tiki Hut Grill." I handed him the gift card. "Welcome to Witch's Cove."

"Thank you. That's very kind of you, ma'am."

Not many things in life really bothered me, except for being called ma'am. "My mom and aunt are ma'ams. I'm just Glinda."

"Sorry, ma'am. I didn't mean to offend."

Steve glared at me. That was my cue to shut up. "No problem," I said. "Do you have a name?"

I felt stupid asking, but he should have offered.

"Nash Solano."

"Deputy Solano, nice to meet you."

"Okay, Glinda," Steve said with a small lift to his lips. "I need Nash to concentrate."

If that wasn't a subtle hint to leave, I don't know what was. Or did he mean I was the distracting type? I inwardly laughed, liking that idea better. "I hear you. I hope to see you around, Deputy Nash."

"Looking forward to it, ma—Glinda."

Not wanting to overstay my welcome, I left. Instead of returning home, I tried to get a view of this agility course for the dogs. After winding my way around a few people, I was able to see what the big hullabaloo was about. The cordoned off area had one dog and two people inside. One person looked like the owner, since he was running alongside of the pooch. The other, a pretty woman, appeared to be a coach of some sort. I will have to say, she had good taste in clothes since she was wearing a pink and white bandana around her neck.

The golden retriever was weaving around poles that jutted up from the ground.

The dog sure did seem to know where to go even without the owner's help—an owner who shouted encouragement. Once through that obstacle, he coaxed the dog to walk on some kind of seesaw. The retriever ran up the plank, waited for the board to change direction, and then ran down. I was impressed. My favorite obstacle was what looked like an accordion tunnel that the dog ran through. The only time the dog slowed down was when he had to jump through a rather small hoop. I was happy to see he executed it with no problem.

The six dogs on the sideline, obediently sitting next to their trainers/owners, appeared to be waiting for their turn to practice. Every once in a while, the pretty female coach would make a suggestion. I could only imagine what the stuffy man who owned Mittens would do when a woman instructed him. He'd scoff for sure and probably tell her he'd been doing these courses far longer than she was alive. I just loved making up stories about people.

As entertaining as this was, I had work to do—as in I needed to find Jaxson and ask for his help. My best male friend's brother was a whiz at the computer. He'd helped with my last case, and I was hoping he might volunteer for another round.

Was it any of my business asking him to research Nash Solano? No, absolutely not, but that didn't mean I wouldn't. I was sure the city council had vetted him inside and out, but even Steve had been friendlier when we first met. That could have been because he'd visited Witch's Cove in the past, and Nash was a first timer.

I did, however, owe my aunt and her helpful friends to learn more about the new deputy. The five gossip queens had been integral to my success in finding who had killed the first deputy and then who had killed Morgan Oliver, nephew to Floyd Paxton, a local rancher.

Happy to get away from the crowd, I walked back toward the Howl at the Moon Cheese and Wine Emporium. I didn't know for sure if Jaxson would be there, but I thought he might be since today was Friday—a busy day for the shop.

After wiping off the mud from my shoes on the entrance mat, I went in. Three people were there. One was browsing, another was asking Drake, the owner, a question, and the third was waiting patiently for a moment of Drake's time. Not wanting to disturb him, I headed to the back without saying anything. If Jaxson wasn't there, I'd exit out the back and head home.

To my delight, Jaxson was hauling in some large boxes from the outside. "Hey," I said. "I thought the delivery men came through the front door."

"Normally he does, but not today for some reason."

I watched Jaxson move gracefully around the counter to the back room. "What's up?" he asked.

I probably shouldn't disturb him when he had a job to do, but after he finished work, he might like to do a little digging.

"I wouldn't say I'm the most intuitive person, but I just met the new deputy," I said.

"Oh, yeah? What's he like?"

From his tone, Jaxson still harbored some ill will toward legal authority. I couldn't blame him since he had spent three years in jail for a crime he hadn't committed.

"Reserved. Or maybe he was just being cautious on his first day."

"Cautious is good. Anything else?"

"That's why I'm here," I said. "If anyone can dig up dirt on him, it's you."

Jaxson's demeanor changed from guarded to pleased. "What's his name?"

"Nash Solano, and he's from Montana. I don't know what town."

"I'll check him out. How many law enforcement men in Montana have that name?"

"I hope only one." I motioned to the shop. "How's it working out with you and Drake?"

He'd been working for his brother for close to two months. I had noticed a positive change in his attitude right after his prison record had been erased, but doing what his little brother asked couldn't have been easy.

"It's good. It's not where I want to be in a year, but for now it brings in a steady paycheck."

"I feel the same way about waitressing."

His brows rose. "Is that so. I thought you loved your job."

"I do, but maybe not for the rest of my life." I wasn't the type to dwell on the future. Most women my age seemed to focus on getting married and settling down. Not me. I wanted to live one day at a time.

"If you could have any job in the world, what would it be?" he asked.

I hadn't taken Jaxson as the dreamer. His brother, on the other hand, was different. "I would work with people in some capacity to help them, which is what I kind of do now."

"It doesn't bother you that you aren't using your education?"

Ah, I could see where this was headed. He had studied some law in school, and then had earned a degree in computer science, and yet he was stacking wine for his brother. "You sound like my parents. Honestly, I try not to think about it. I do know that teaching school isn't for me."

"So, what would make you happy—taking money out of the equation?"

Where was he going with this? Was he that unsettled with his life and this was a projection of his own desires? "I'm not unhappy now, so that's not an easy question. But if I have to answer, I'd say I could see myself as a private investigator of some sort, though I wouldn't enjoy putting my life on the line like Steve does." I smiled. "Now it's your turn."

"I've been asking myself that question every day and still haven't come up with an answer."

I thought it was rather obvious. "You like finding information on the computer."

"I do," Jaxson said. "The problem is that I want to have a say in what I research, which was why becoming a lawyer wasn't for me."

"Good to know."

He smiled. "If you ever figure out what I would excel at, let me know."

I laughed. "I need to find my calling first."

"Good luck with that, Glinda."

Happy to have done my civic duty by spying on the newcomer and getting to know Jaxson better, I was ready to go home and relax. And by relax, I meant filling Iggy and my aunt in on what I'd found out before indulging in a glass of wine and maybe watching some mindless television show.

Chapter Three

BECAUSE THE TIKI Hut was really busy the next day, I had considered helping out, but since it was my unscheduled day off, I had several things I needed to attend to. Thankfully, Corinne, who was a competent server, would be inside with Penny, and one of the evening shift folks would switch to the day shift on the patio. It would be chaotic for sure, but yesterday had been hectic too. I suspected tomorrow, the day of the show, would be worse, since more visitors would be arriving.

As I gathered my stuff to head out to the dog show, someone knocked on my apartment door. I looked over at Iggy. "Did you invite anyone?" I asked, not really thinking he had.

"No."

The only way to find out the identity of my guest was to look. The peephole revealed Gertrude Poole there, hunched over, with one hand on the door jam. Whoa. I never expected her. I pulled it open.

Gertrude was the ancient psychic and former spell master who helped me find Morgan Oliver's killer. She was panting heavily, which I understood. The stairs leading up to my place were long and steep. They would be especially difficult for someone close to ninety. "Gertrude, come in and sit down."

"Thank you." She grabbed my arm to steady herself. I led her over to the sofa and guided her to a seat.

"Can I get you anything? Water, iced tea, coffee?"

"I know it's early, but do you have any spirits?" The twinkle in her eye was unmistakable.

By spirits, I assumed she meant alcohol. It would have to be wine since I didn't drink hard liquor. "A bit of chardonnay perhaps?"

She smiled, and her face looked twenty years younger. "That would be wonderful."

As I hurried into the kitchen to fix her a glass, Iggy jumped down from his perch and rushed over to Gertrude. I could hear the two of them chatting, but I wasn't able to make out what they were saying. Iggy had snuck out last month to speak with her about Morgan Oliver's death, and the intel he'd learned from her had been invaluable.

It was always nice for Iggy to find someone other than myself and Aunt Fern to chat with.

Since I was in the kitchen already, I made myself a glass of sweet tea and then gathered a few arugula leaves for Iggy. I returned to the living room with a tray containing his plate as well as both of our drinks. I set the tray down on the coffee table and then handed Gertrude her wine and put Iggy's small plate on the coffee table. I hoped her need for the spirits wasn't because she wanted to tell me something that I would find unpleasant. I then placed the tray next to my chair to get it out of the way.

I sat down next to the sofa. "How can I help you?"

"I had a vision."

Considering she was a psychic, I figured she often had them. I was just glad she didn't say someone had died and that she needed my help in finding the killer.

Iggy jumped on the coffee table, careful to avoid the glasses and munched on his treat. He always liked to be in the middle of any conversation.

"What kind of vision?" I asked.

"A pink one."

I almost laughed. I've never had a vision, but if I did, I always imagined one of mine would be pink. "Other than the color, what does it have to do with me?" I prayed it didn't show harm coming my way.

"Visions aren't exact science, mind you. They are often cryptic and open to interpretation."

Like Gertrude was being right now. "What was in this vision?"

"Have you been to the park to see the dogs practice for the competition?"

I thought she was about to talk about her vision. If her mind was going, it would be a terrible shame for the witch community at large. "I have. Have you?"

I would never have guessed she'd have had the stamina to walk the several blocks from the Psychics Corner to the Tiki Hut Grill let alone go to the park, though it was possible someone had driven her.

"No, which is why I thought my vision was rather strange." She took a large drink of her wine.

Gertrude seemed to like to draw out a story. "What exactly did you see?" I asked.

"One of the dogs in the show had a pink aura around it."

A pink aura? I'd never heard of anything like that before. Then again, I had little experience with psychic visions. "And you thought of me, because I only wear pink?"

"I did."

My thoughts shot in many directions. "Do you think I had something to do with the creation of the aura?" I'm not sure I could have made one even if I had tried. I wasn't the luckiest witch when it came to spells.

"I have no idea," she said.

This wasn't getting us anywhere. "What does an aura signify?" I asked.

She shrugged and then downed the rest of her wine. Oh, my. "It could be that dog is in danger, or it might mean the animal is destined for greatness. Visions don't come with an instruction manual, you know. They are like dreams in a way. You have to interpret them."

That was her forte, not mine. It appeared as if I wasn't a key player in her vision then, for which I was thankful. I was curious to know more though. "What did the dog look like? There are seven who are competing."

"It was a Border Collie."

Mittens, the dog owned by the well-dressed but standoff-ish man, was a Border Collie. "Should I warn the owner?"

Gertrude stared off into space and then returned her gaze to me. "I don't know. I'm here merely to tell you what I saw."

That wasn't very helpful. "I shouldn't take any action then?" If not, why come and tell me?

She smiled and then rose slowly to her feet—a sure sign that our time together was over. "Do what you always do."

"What is that?"

"Investigate."

Oh, my. I stood too. Gertrude shuffled toward the door. Fearful she might fall going down the stairs, I wrapped an arm around her waist and helped her.

"Is someone here to drive you back to your office?" Or did she have some amazing powers none of us were aware of— like having the ability to teleport?

"I'll walk dear. I might even wander over to the park."

I was too stunned to respond. The trip would be close to a mile. "Let me know if you find out something."

"You too, dear."

With that last farewell, Gertrude turned right to exit through the restaurant. I didn't watch to see if she stopped to speak with Aunt Fern or not. My head wasn't in the right space for that.

I hurried upstairs, trying to decide if I should tell anyone. There hadn't been a crime committed, so there was no need to bother the sheriff or his deputy, and Penny would be too busy right now to discuss my next move.

What concerned me the most was that Gertrude had never come to me before, and I had to believe she'd had many visions. Why now? Was the color pink the only reason she met with me? Or was there something worth investigating with this Border Collie and his master that even she was unaware of?

Darn. Just when I'd sworn off interfering, the queen of witches showed up, asking for my help. It wasn't as if I could say no. I owed her one. While I wasn't active in our coven, turning down Gertrude Poole would be frowned upon.

In order to investigate though, I'd need help. As in I

needed to know the name of Mittens' owner so that Jaxson could look into him to make sure he wasn't some criminal. Knowing that information would give me some peace of mind. I figured there had to be a record of the owner's name somewhere.

I mentally snapped my fingers. Of course! Eleanor Aldrich, the event coordinator, would know the names of all of the owners. I'd locate her, ask for the information, and then talk to Jaxson. Phew.

Eleanor lived on the far end of town on a large, horse breeding farm that she and her husband owned. Before I drove out there, I decided to check the park first. I would think she'd want to be aware of everything that was going on for the three-day event.

I grabbed my keys and phone.

"Where are you going?" Iggy asked. "We need to discuss this vision."

"What is there to discuss? Even Gertrude doesn't know what it means. I can't do much unless something comes of it."

"I know you. You have a plan. What is it?"

Could the little bugger read my mind? We were magically connected, so maybe he could.

I told him about needing to find Eleanor and then asking Jaxson to dig up some dirt on the owner. "I would consider taking you with me, but if one of the dogs came around to snoop, he might think you'd make a tasty snack."

Iggy lifted up his body. "You're making that up."

Only partially. "It's possible, but I promise we'll chat when I know something, okay?"

He plopped down on his stomach. "You always say that."

"Because it's true."

I didn't have time to debate this. I darted out, flew down the stairs, and went outside. Looking at the number of people out and about made it look more like Christmastime than the middle of summer. Most of the shops were full of people, probably because standing in the hot sun for a few hours would be hard for all but us seasoned Floridians.

As soon as I arrived, I spotted Steve and assumed Nash was somewhere nearby. I walked over to our esteemed sheriff. "Hey, there," I said, trying to sound friendly but not too nosy. "I met one of the dog owners at the restaurant this morning, and he left something behind."

I had no idea why I just lied, but I wanted to have a reason for everything I did—other than me being my usual snoopy self.

"Is that so?"

I had the sense he didn't believe me. Darn his smooth, controlled voice. I bet he used it often to cover up his true feelings. "Do you know where Eleanor Aldrich is? I'm sure she has the list of owners."

Steve pulled a folded piece of paper from his top pocket. "You can have my list of names, but if you wouldn't mind, make me a copy and then return this?"

That was easy. "Sure thing! I'll drop it off later."

In truth, I didn't need the man's name to return the item—an item that only existed in my mind. I needed it to do research.

"Glinda, are you sure that's the only reason you want the list?" One brow rose. Darn. He knew I was fibbing.

I was such a bad liar, which meant I might as well tell him

the truth. Before I could though, some people watching the festivities gasped, and Steve's attention was immediately drawn to the commotion.

"Excuse me," he said as he jogged away.

That was a lucky break. The increase in chatter made me want to see what was happening too. I followed Steve but at a discreet distance. Only when I was near enough to the dogs did my breath catch, forcing me to lock my knees to keep from dropping to the ground. The Border Collie had a pink glow about him—just like in Gertrude's vision!

Steve stopped to speak with a couple who were pointing excitedly at the dog. Wanting to stay out of their discussion, two of the local witches were also chatting about this unusual phenomenon. They, however, were speaking in a more subdued manner, acting as if this was an everyday occasion.

I moved in. "Hey, Regina and Cassie. What's going on?"

"Oh, Glinda. Look." She pointed to Mittens. "You see it right?"

"The pink aura around the dog?" They nodded. "I do, but his owner doesn't seem to have a clue, does he?" In truth, the owner had acted so reserved at the restaurant, I'm not sure he'd react even if he could see the aura.

"I doubt it, which is why I think maybe only our kind can detect it."

That made sense. "What do you think it means?" Gertrude didn't seem to know, so there was no reason to bring up her name.

"I'm thinking it's a sign that this one is going to win," Regina said with a smile that reached her eyes.

"Wouldn't that be nice if we had a symbol like that all the

time? We witches could clean up at the gambling table." I was mostly kidding.

"Who needs a gambling table? You can bet on the dogs right here," Cassie piped up.

Now I was interested. "Really? I thought that was illegal."

"From what I've heard, it is, unless it meets some specific town requirements. I'm not up on the details, but I know that a large portion of the winnings will go to the animal shelter. Since it's a charity thing, people can bet. Talk to Bob Hatfield. He's in charge. Last time I saw him, he was on the other side of the training course."

I didn't really want to bet, but I was curious to learn what was going on. I wouldn't mention it to the sheriff in case Cassie's information was wrong. "I think I will. If you'll excuse me, ladies, I need to talk to someone." Namely, Mittens' owner.

I slipped away from them and then consulted the piece of paper that contained the names of the dogs and the identity of their owners. The Border Collie was owned by Josh Randall. I never would have guessed he'd be a dog person though. To be fair, just because he didn't seem to be able to connect with people didn't mean he wasn't a good owner.

I slowly walked around the roped off area looking for him. Mittens had finished his session, because now a Jack Russell Terrier was in his place. I watched for a bit since this event was truly fascinating. I had to say, this dog looked really good, though I hadn't seen enough of the sport to compare one dog to another.

After moving away from the roped off area, I scoured the rest of the park for Josh and Mittens. They couldn't have gone far since they'd just left the arena.

Would Josh take his dog straight to the hotel, or was Mittens encouraged to run around and play with the other dogs? Loud barking off to the side caught my attention, so I headed over there. The fenced off area was full of dogs having fun. That came as no surprise as that was the doggie park.

After a full sweep of the area, I wasn't able to see where Josh Randall had disappeared to. The big question was whether he had seen the pink aura for himself. If so, did he know what it meant?

Chapter Four

ONCE I WAS convinced that the pink aura dog and his owner weren't in the park, I headed back to the main part of town. I needed to find out what Jaxson had learned about our deputy and then ask for another favor. Normally, I wouldn't have involved him so much, but after our earlier conversation, I sensed that Jaxson was looking for something to do that was more important than ordering wine.

Even though it was Saturday, the shop wasn't as crowded as I'd expected. However, it was lunch hour, which meant people might be eating. Hopefully, they intended to buy their wine after the dog training session was done for the day.

I merely waved to Drake since he was with a customer and then headed to the back once more. I felt bad not talking to him since he was my friend. Tomorrow, the shop was closed. After I finished my shift, I'd see about meeting up with him.

Jaxson was in the back doing his thing, and he smiled when he spotted me. "How's my favorite sleuth?" he said.

"It's been a crazy day, but first tell me what you've learned about Nash Solano." Jaxson wasn't the type to procrastinate. He would have looked stuff up last night.

"It's rather odd," he said. "The guy is almost a ghost. I

printed something off for you to check out. I want to make sure I have the right person." Jaxson ducked into the storage closet and then handed me a piece of paper.

It was a side view of Nash in a spiffy-looking dress uniform, receiving some kind of award. "That's him. Is this the only shot you have of him?"

"Yes. While his name is everywhere on the sheriff's department website, he seems to have been missing during every photo session."

"I find that strange, too, though I've met people who are camera shy." Considering Nash could get a modeling gig in a heartbeat, I didn't understand the avoidance. "Did you find out why he was avoiding detection?"

"Not yet. He has a lot of commendations, indicating he's quite an accomplished law enforcement agent. I learned that he took some online courses to be eligible to work in Florida."

"Interesting. Duncan Donut didn't step down until a month ago, which meant the opening wouldn't have been posted until after that." Just last week, our town held an election, and Steve was voted in as our new sheriff. Considering he ran unopposed, the whole thing was a waste of money, but I understood the need for protocol.

"Nash must have been thinking about relocating for a while. When the opening came up, he jumped on it." Jaxson said. "Maybe he was planning to get away from the weather."

"Could be." I might never know. Hopefully, Pearl could worm more information out of him. "While I really appreciate your investigation, I would like you to divert your attention elsewhere."

Jaxson's eyes widened. "That sounds interesting."

I detailed my discussion with Gertrude and how several of us saw the pink aura around Mittens. "I might have ignored the vision if Gertrude hadn't made such a big deal of it."

He leaned his elbows on the waist high counter. "What do you make of it?" he asked.

"That Mittens is a winner maybe? But the only way for the aura to mean that would be if a witch put some kind of spell on the dog for that express purpose."

He chuckled. "I'd like to see Steve Rocker prove that the owner was able to earn a lot of money from the betting pool because of a spell."

I explained that most of the money went to charity. "Since Steve is a bit skeptical when it comes to the occult, I would have to agree with you that he'd dismiss it. How about I check with a few witches while you focus on Josh Randall? Something like this might have happened before."

Jaxson scribbled down the name. "Got it. Anything else, boss?"

I laughed. "I'm not your boss, because I'm not paying you."

"That's a shame."

"You know I would if I could." Even though my room and board were basically free, thanks to my aunt's generosity, my wages weren't great—though I made more waitressing than teaching.

"Hey, could Josh be a warlock?" Jaxson asked.

"Anything's possible, but just so you know, I can't tell if a person is a warlock or a witch. They'd have to tell me."

"Good to know."

With Jaxson promising to get on the investigation as soon

as he could, I walked over to the Psychics Corner. Our town had a lot of witches and warlocks, many of whom were probably at the dog park, but discussing some things in public probably wouldn't be smart.

I mentally ran through the list of those who charged for their services. Just because Mindy Wilson was a palm reader or Brittany DeWitt was a fortune teller, it didn't mean they didn't have other talents. I couldn't remember if anyone used their abilities to do spells—other than a few love potions. I mentally snapped my fingers. Claire Voyant—not her real name—performed séances. Because most of her clients preferred to hold sessions at night, she might be free now. She had performed a spell or two for some of the locals, so someone might have hired her to do this pink aura one.

For a moment, I had considered going back to the Hex and Bones apothecary where I'd purchased the ingredients to change Iggy back to green. I'd ask if anyone knew about pink auras. Considering the owner had yet to return from visiting her sister, I thought it might be best to avoid Hazel, who'd messed up the last time.

As I entered the Psychics Corner, considering all of the tourists in town, I expected to see the waiting room packed. Instead, it was almost empty. Thankfully, their receptionist, Sarah, was there and could help me.

"Hey, Glinda. This is a surprise. What can I do for you?"

"I'm looking for someone who might be able to tell me about auras."

"As in an aura cleansing?" she asked.

"No." Since Gertrude worked here, I had no problem discussing her vision. "She had no idea what the pink aura meant, so I headed over to the park to check out the dogs."

The receptionist's eyes opened wide. "Don't tell me you saw Mittens with a pink aura?"

"I did, as did a few others. Not everyone could see it, though. I'm thinking a witch put some kind of spell on the dog. Do you know of anyone who might be aware of something like that? Claire Voyant perhaps?"

She sat there for a moment, drumming her fingers. "Claire doesn't come in until later. How about Jack Hanson?"

I'd met him a few times, and he seemed like a nice guy. "I thought he only did tarot card readings. Does he do spells too?"

"Yes, but he would never do anything to harm anyone."

That wasn't what I was implying. "I'm sure he wouldn't. Is he in?"

"Let me check." After consulting with the calendar on her computer, she nodded. "Yes. Go down the hall. He's the third door on the right."

"Thanks," I said.

"I'll let him know you're coming."

Despite this whole aura thing not being any of my business, I couldn't ignore something this exciting. It wasn't often one was able to see a visual representation of a spell.

At Jack's door, I knocked and entered. The windowless room was small but cozy. Tapestries hung on the walls, and antique-looking lamps sat on side tables. I wouldn't be surprised if he had a smoke machine in the corner for when a client showed up. That would provide an other-world feel.

About the only cliché he wasn't employing was that he didn't dress up as some kind of bohemian. In truth, I don't think he could have pulled it off. Jack was too rugged a man to be wearing a head scarf adorned with dangling silver and gold metal discs.

He smiled. "Glinda, welcome."

Good thing the receptionist had typed my name into his calendar since I don't think we'd seen each other since before I left for college. I had to assume he wasn't a fan of the Tiki Hut food since I'd never served him. "Thank you."

"How can I help?" he asked. "I'm assuming you didn't come for a tarot card reading."

"No."

I took the offered seat and jumped right into the reason for my visit. I explained about Gertrude's vision and about my seeing the pink aura around the dog. I also mentioned the other two witches who saw the same thing.

"What can I do?"

"I was hoping you might know if the aura was placed there by a witch. If so, for what purpose?"

Jack leaned back in his chair. "I've never heard of a witch or warlock talking about anything like that, but it's possible. Do you know if this aura represents something good or something evil?"

That would be helpful to know. "It means nothing at the moment. People are speculating it might mean that dog is destined to win."

"I wish I could help you. Unless you learn of its purpose, I'm at a loss as to who might have created it."

Well, that was a bust—sort of. "I appreciate you taking the time to see me."

Since he had spent a few minutes with me, I offered to

pay, but he declined.

"Figuring out the answer will be good enough pay for me," he said. "This has me intrigued."

"Me too." I smiled. "Deal a few cards. Maybe they will tell you something."

He chuckled. "Maybe they will."

I left, trying to figure out my next move. Because the first eating establishment I would pass was the Spellbound Diner, I decided to grab a bite to eat and see what Dolly knew.

As soon as I walked in, I could see this might take a while. Every booth was taken. While I wasn't the wait-in-line type, I didn't have a choice if I wanted to pick Dolly's brain. I would have snagged her for a chat, but she was running around taking orders and delivering food like a mad woman. I wouldn't be surprised if she was helping to cook too.

Twenty minutes later, I was finally seated. I probably should have offered to share a booth with some stranger, but what I had to say to Dolly needed to be done in private.

It wasn't long before one of the servers came over to my booth. I ordered a sweet iced tea and a grilled cheese sandwich, only this time I asked for it with a slice of ham and tomato. "I know Dolly is really busy, but if she has a chance, I'd like to chat."

The server grinned. "More gossip?"

I laughed. "You understand, I see."

Dolly came over in less than a minute with my tea in hand and slid in across from me. "What do you have for me?"

As briefly as I could, I described Gertrude's visit and my viewing of the pink aura. I even told her about my request to Jaxson to find out about Josh Randall. Lastly, I mentioned my visit to Jack Hanson. "And here I am."

"I had heard about the aura, but it's been so busy in here that I haven't had a chance to talk to anyone else." As if the gossip gods were listening, her cell rang. As she checked it, a broad smile appeared. "It's Pearl."

"Answer it." This could be big.

"Pearl, hon, I'm a bit busy. Uh-huh. What? When?"

I watched Dolly's face intently. Something had happened, but I couldn't tell how bad it was. She finally hung up. "Well, I'll be."

"What?"

"You know that dog with the pink aura around him?"

Of course, I did. I just told her about him. "Yes?"

"He's gone missing."

Chapter Five

THE LAST THING I expected to learn from my visit to Dolly's diner was that Mittens was missing. "Was it a runaway kind of missing or a kidnapped kind of missing?"

"I don't know. Pearl just said that a distraught owner came into the station to report his missing dog. Mittens is scheduled to compete tomorrow, and the owner is frantic."

"That would be Josh Randall. I can only imagine the fuss he made. I doubt he would have been polite about his demands to Steve either, asking that the sheriff drop everything and find his precious dog. Though if someone took Iggy, I'd be irrational too."

"I get it."

Darn. This meant I needed to copy the list of names and return it to Steve so he could investigate the other competitors—not that he couldn't call Eleanor again for the list, but why should he have to?

When my cell buzzed, I could guess who it was. I checked the screen. Yup, maybe I am a bit psychic. "Hi, Steve. I will return the list in a second. I'm just finishing lunch."

"How did you know why I was calling?" he asked, suspicion coloring his tone.

I chuckled. "You don't know by now that half the town is

aware of the missing dog? The owner has probably accused the other dog owners of being jealous, which is why one of them took Mittens. He'll tell you his dog is the best and was going to win."

Silence followed. "Wow. I've underestimated you."

I had to smile. "I know. Be over in a bit."

"Okay, thank you."

I disconnected. Dolly was shaking her head. "When will the law in this town realize we are a great source of help?"

"You are so right. Speaking of which, do you have a piece of paper I could have? It could even be a sheet out of an order pad."

"Sure thing." She pulled her pad from her pocket, tore off a piece and handed it to me.

"I need to get something to Steve ASAP, so could I have the grilled cheese to go?"

Dolly smiled. "Coming right up."

After I copied the list of names for myself, grabbed my To-Go bag and paid, I darted across the street to the sheriff's office. When I entered, I was a bit surprised to find both Steve and Nash there. One, if not both, should have been out looking for the missing dog—or was that the job of the dog catcher? Clearly, I wasn't well-versed in law enforcement protocol.

I waved Steve's original list at Pearl as I came in. "Steve lent something to me that I need to return. He just called."

"By all means." She motioned for me to enter the inner sanctum.

I wasn't sure why the office seemed different. It might have been because of the increased level of testosterone. The place exuded a vibe that said all nosy waitresses needed to stay clear—but that didn't mean I would.

Steve was talking with Nash when I approached. He stopped, looked up, and nodded to the paper in my hand. "Thanks for returning it. Learn anything?" he asked.

I gave him his original list. "As a matter of fact, I have. Kind of. Not who took the dog though."

He pulled two seats in front of his old desk—a desk that now belonged to Nash and sat down, motioning for me to do the same. "Tell us."

Oh, boy. It had been hard enough convincing Steve that I had some powers. Now I'd have to explain myself to the Montana cowboy here—or should I say to the highly decorated Montanan.

I turned to Steve. "I don't know if you saw it or not, but several of us witches spotted a pink aura around Mittens as he was practicing the agility course."

"That was what the two women I spoke to told me," Steve said. "I saw the dog but no pink aura of any kind."

Nash leaned forward. "Hold on a second. You actually saw the pink aura?" he asked.

"I did, but since I'm a witch, and the others who saw the aura were also witches, I'm guessing it was something only we could see."

"How about describing this aura for us? I want to see if it matches what those ladies told me," Steve said.

What was there to describe? Saying it was pink would be too obvious. "The dog had about a six-inch ring of light around his body. It stayed with the dog wherever it went."

"Do you know how it got there?" Steve asked.

"I wish I did, but it wasn't from lack of trying to learn about such auras." I explained about my trip to Jack Hanson's office. "He wasn't able to point any fingers either, mostly because he didn't know if the spell was a good one or not. With the dog's disappearance, I'm guessing a not-so-nice witch was paid to do this."

"Any guesses as to who?" Steve asked.

"Nope. I'm not exactly an active member of our coven. From what I've been told, the ones who do evil spells aren't the real social type, if you get my drift."

"I see," Steve said.

"And before you ask, even if I met all of the other contestants, I couldn't tell if a person is a witch or not—evil or otherwise."

"Good to know. Is your inability to spot another witch specific to you or to all witches?" Nash asked.

"I believe it's to all witches, though I haven't spoken to every single one of them. There is no 'visible-only-to-witches' stamp on our forehead that indicates who is and who isn't a witch. To be honest, if they don't work at the Psychics Corner and have a sign on their door indicating their talent, we don't really talk much about what we can and can't do."

Nash kept his gaze on me. It was almost as if he believed that if he looked hard enough, he could read my mind.

"Are you saying that trying to locate this spell person would be a waste of time then?" Nash asked.

I appreciated that he didn't dismiss me as a kook right off. "Probably. The woman who told me about the aura is rather old, but at one time, she was the most powerful witch in town. If she didn't know who created it, I doubt anyone does."

Steve stretched out his legs as he shifted in his chair. The man was too big for sitting. "Your grapevine ladies didn't say who might have taken the pooch?"

"No, but you should ask Pearl."

Steve smiled. "I believe you called her one of the five gossip queens?"

"I did. I call it like I see it." I glanced between the men. "Is there anything you think I can do to help? I'm not really a dog person, because I have Iggy."

"Iggy?" Nash asked.

"My pink iguana. He's a big hit with the ladies." If either knew I could talk with him, they'd kick me out or lock me up.

"Just do what you do best," Steve said.

Why did people always say that? "You mean ask questions?"

"Yes. People see our uniforms and clam up. You seem to have a golden touch when it comes to finding out stuff."

My pulse rocketed at those kind words. I had a golden touch. How about that? "I can do that. If you want me to know something—"

"I know," Steve said. "I'll call."

"That wasn't what I was going to say. I meant, tell Pearl."

This time he laughed.

On my way out, I chatted with her for a minute and then went back to my place. I had a grilled cheese sandwich to eat and a curious iguana to fill in on what happened—assuming he hadn't learned about it already.

Once home, I scarfed down my sandwich. In between bites, I told Iggy everything.

"Gertrude proves to be the real deal once more," Iggy said.

"You can say that again. I am highly impressed with her talents. You've never had any kind of aura placed around you, have you?" I asked.

"Not that I know of. I think I'm pink enough," he said. This time his tone held no bitterness.

I laughed. "Yes, you are. And I love that you are. It shows you are secure in your skin."

He looked at me a bit funny. "Like I have a choice? I know what you are trying to do."

I knew too. I wanted him to feel good about himself. "That's because you are smart. I have a job for you and maybe for Aimee too."

He lifted up. "What's that?"

"Someone must know what's going on. I'd like you to do your detective thing and snoop around. Too often people are so absorbed in what they are doing that they don't notice a small, pink iguana running around."

"Cool. I can do that."

"But don't go to the park. Not only is it really far away, there are so many people there that you might get trampled," I said.

"You're no fun."

"There are a ton of people downstairs. Listen in on their conversations, but try not to scare them. The tourists might freak out if they notice you."

I'd purposefully put a pink rhinestone collar on him to prevent people from thinking he was some wild animal.

"Fine." Iggy didn't sound fine, but it couldn't be helped.

I dumped my plate in the sink and grabbed my gear once more. No rest for the weary. "I think I'll have a little chat with Hazel to see if anyone purchased ingredients that could be used for a pink aura spell."

"Do you trust her? I mean, look what happened to us?"

"I'm out of options, but it'll be fine. I'm not there for a spell." While there, I'd like to find that spell, in part because the books might indicate its intended use.

"Are you sure you don't want to take me with you?" Iggy asked.

"It won't be fun for you. After I speak with Hazel, I need to ask Jaxson for some help."

Instead of responding, he waddled over to his stool and hopped on top. I hoped he wouldn't sulk for long. I needed some intel from the customers downstairs.

At the Hex and Bones Apothecary, I was delighted to find that Bertha Murdoch, the owner, had returned from visiting with her sick sister.

Considering the big event going on, it shouldn't have surprised me that the store was quite crowded. I was happy for her. I hope Bertha made a ton of money during this three-day dog show. She must have expected the rush because Hazel was there too. While her presence was a bit unexpected given her last goof, I was fine with it.

In the end, the pink potion fiasco turned out okay. Iggy seemed to have come to terms with always being pink. Looking back on it, I think he just wanted me to try to get the potion to show him that I cared.

Since both women were busy, I stopped over at the table with the spell books. Most visitors would assume they were there for show, but I knew better. The only negative to physical books was the poor table of contents. If these books had been online, it would have been easy to search for a pink aura spell.

I pulled out a chair, ready to investigate. One of my issues was that I have a bit of attention deficit disorder. Even though I'd come with the express purpose of finding a particular spell, the variety of items in this book was too exciting not to look at them. I had to read a few. Okay, a lot more than a few.

"Glinda?"

I spun around and breathed a sigh of relief. It was Bertha. I pushed back my chair, stood, and hugged her. "I'm glad you are back. How is your sister?"

"She's slowly improving."

When she didn't elaborate, I figured it would be better not to ask. "I suppose you've heard about the missing dog?"

"Of course. It's such a shame. I have a schnauzer at home. If anyone took him, I'd be a basket case."

"I could say the same if anyone took Iggy. Did you hear about the pink aura around the dog shortly before he disappeared?"

"I did."

I had hoped she'd offer her opinion, but she didn't. "Do you know of any spells in these books that could create such an aura?" What I really wanted to ask was if she knew who might have been responsible for it.

"I imagine there are, but no one has come in and asked about it. That being said, they could have spoken with Hazel, or they might have bought the ingredients without mentioning what they were going to be used for."

That was what I was afraid of. "You don't recall seeing such a spell?"

"My dear, I might have spent most of my life studying them, but even I don't know every spell. You should ask Gertrude Poole. Now there is a woman who would know."

"She's the one who told me about it, but she wasn't sure of its purpose," I said.

"I see."

"If you hear anything, will you let me know?" I'd let her deal with Hazel and ask her.

"I definitely will. As soon as I have time, I will do some research. If we know its purpose, it might give us a clue why someone needed it."

"I totally agree," I said. "However, we have no way of knowing if the pink aura is related to the missing dog or not."

"That is true. Let's just hope the dog comes back soon so we don't have to worry about it."

"It's what we all want. And thanks."

My next stop was to tell Jaxson and Drake about the missing dog. With the amount of traffic he'd probably have today, I wanted them to keep their ears open.

Chapter Six

"GLINDA, I'M SORRY," Jaxson said the moment I stepped into the back room. "I haven't had the chance to research many of the names on your list of contestants."

"That's okay. It's not exactly why I'm here. In case you haven't heard, the dog with the pink aura around it went missing."

Drake followed me in right after the doorbell chimed, which indicated his customers had left. "What's this about a missing dog?"

"Mittens is missing."

"Really? That's a shame, but finding lost pups is not your usual fare," Drake said.

I'd been involved in two whole cases, even though I wasn't some private eye or anything. "I will admit that the last two times I was obsessed with helping someone, it involved a murder. Unless you know of some hidden dead body, I'm going to look into the missing dog," I said.

That got a smile out of him. "I've owned one or two dogs in my life, and trust me, both of mine would go off and explore all the time," Drake said. "Butch went missing for two days once before he came back happy as a clam."

"I'm glad, but these dogs are well-trained. I don't think

they'd just wander off. If one of them did become distracted or something, he'd return when the owner called him." Or so I believed. "The missing dog was the one who had a pink aura around him."

"Oh. That changes things. You don't find it coincidental that it was a *pink* aura?" Drake asked.

"It's not what you think. I didn't imagine it. A bunch of other witches saw it too." I explained that Steve was even investigating it. "I just came from speaking with him since I had to return the list of contestants I'd borrowed. I saw him make a report on their sighting. When I asked him about it, Steve claimed he saw the dog but not the aura."

"It's a witch thing then?" Jaxson asked.

"Apparently."

"What does this aura have to do with the missing dog?" Drake asked.

"I don't know. Maybe nothing. All I know is that one minute the dog had this aura around it, and the next he's gone. Coincidence? Or even correlated? I don't know."

"Let's ignore the aura for now," Jaxson said. "Let's assume that someone kidnapped the dog. Are you thinking another competitor took the dog so their animal would have a better chance of winning?"

"It's a thought," I said. "But there are seven dogs in the show, all different breeds. While I am no expert, no one could mistake one for the other," I said. "No aura should be needed."

Jaxson pulled something out of his pocket. "I printed a picture of each breed of dog as well as the pictures of each of their owners." He placed them flat on the table.

Drake studied the dog photo. "You have a point. It would be hard to nab the wrong one, but I repeat. This is assuming someone took the dog. Dogs do run away."

"I realize that," I said, "but why would someone put a spell on a dog? If any contestant was involved, there'd be no need. They would have nabbed the correct dog. Or am I overthinking this?"

"I think you're right," Jaxson said. "The aura would have to be used as a signal for someone else."

"Which means the dognapper—assuming that was what happened—had to have been a witch or a warlock. Otherwise, he or she couldn't have seen the aura," Drake said.

"I agree," I said. "Here's a thought. It is possible, the aura wasn't to identify the dog, but rather to subdue the dog."

"What do you mean?" Drake asked.

"While I have never heard of a spell like this, maybe it's some kind of hypnotic spell that makes it so that the dog will follow anyone with a certain scent or who gives a certain command."

Jaxson and Drake looked at each other, probably trying to decide if I truly was crazy. "Can you find out if such a spell exists?"

"I can try."

"If we can learn why the dog was taken—again, assuming he was—it might help us figure out who was responsible," Drake said.

That reason for the spell seemed to be a sticking point. "Any suggestions where I should look?" I asked.

The two brothers looked at each other. "Other than going back to speak with a fellow witch, I got nothing," Jaxson said.

"My neither. You said you were just with our sheriff. He's not looking for the dog?" Drake asked.

"It didn't look like it. Both he and Nash were at the station a few minutes ago."

Jaxson held up a finger. "I'll check out the dog owners to see if something like this has happened to them before."

I snapped my fingers. "You are a genius."

Jaxson tapped his chest. "Me?"

"When I spoke to the owner of the Papillon, apparently this show wasn't for first timers. She claimed it was some kind of Master's level competition."

Drake smiled. "And you want to know which competitions, if any, had any reports of stolen pets. We could then cross-reference which of our seven contestants were also at the same events. If so, that might narrow the field."

"Exactly. Unfortunately, I know nothing about these dog competitions. I'm hoping my good friend who works at the library can help."

"It's worth a shot," Drake said.

After I thanked them again for their help, I walked next door to the parking lot since the library was a distance away. Just as I reached my car, my cell rang. It was my mother. Guilt hit me once more. Every time I became wrapped up in helping someone, I didn't make the time to see my parents.

"Hi, Mom."

"Glinda, I'm sure you're off helping someone, but I wanted to remind you about your father's birthday dinner on Monday."

My heart nearly stopped. I had forgotten. It was his fiftieth birthday, which made it a big deal. At least I had purchased his gifts already. "Sure. What time do you want me?"

"Seven at our place?"

"Sure. What can I bring?" I asked.

"Don't you remember you said you'd make the cranberry sauce and that yummy yam casserole?"

The memory came flooding back. "Absolutely. Seven o'clock. Monday. Be there. Thanks, Mom."

"Is everything okay, sweetie? You sound, oh, I don't know, more stressed than usual."

I didn't want to burden her with this dog mess. She'd want to know why I was getting involved with something that was none of my business. Again. At some point, I'd have to tell her about the request from Gertrude Poole. Even my mother wouldn't have turned down Gertrude. She was a valued member of our coven—a coven to which I never considered myself belonging. "I'm fine. I'm off to the library. See you in two days. Love you."

"Love you too." Her voice faded, most likely from worry.

I hopped in my car and drove to the library. When I walked in, I was happy to see Delilah Smithson manning the front desk. She'd helped so much on the Morgan Oliver case that I was hoping she could steer me in the right direction for this one.

When I approached, Delilah looked up from her computer and smiled. "Well, well. This is becoming a habit. I love it."

"It seems to be. Since you lent me your genius before, I was hoping you could help me again," I said.

"I'd love to try. What do you need?"

I explained everything from the pink aura to the missing

dog. "In case this type of thing has happened before in Florida, I'd like a list of cities that have hosted agility competitions in say, the last six months."

"I can certainly take a look," she said.

"I plan to ask Sheriff Rocker to check for reports of missing dogs in these cities during the run of the show."

"Sounds good. Give me a few minutes, okay?"

"Sure." I left Delilah to do her thing while I did a bit of research on my own. I found out that there were classes of competition for this stuff from novice to master level. These dogs at our show must be the best of the best then. I also learned what the obstacles were called. There were weave poles, seesaws, and open tunnels to name a few. Apparently, there could be anywhere from fourteen to twenty obstacles per event. This was a whole new world to me that I found quite fascinating.

Twenty minutes later, Delilah came over with a print out. "I have the list of agility competitions you want."

When I looked at the list, I sank down in my chair. "Are you kidding me? There's been about one every week." I'd been hoping for once a month. I scanned the list. "I'm sure there will be no mention of missing dogs though. If there were, no one would enter. At least I know the location of the towns, so thank you."

While I could ask Jaxson to investigate these, it would be easier to see what Steve could pull up.

"You don't have to come just for research, you know," Delilah said.

"I know. Time seems to get away from me, and life gets in the way sometimes."

She smiled. "I hear you."

With the list of events in hand, I returned to the sheriff's department. This time, the only law enforcement person there was Nash. I didn't want to discriminate, so I asked Pearl if I could speak with him.

"Of course, dear. I'm sure he'll make time for you."

As I walked toward the back, Nash looked up. While he said nothing, his eyes screamed surprise.

He nodded to the paper in my hand. "What's that?"

I handed him the print out. "I've been doing some brain-storming and was wondering if maybe there have been other missing dogs at previous agility events. I have a list of all of the competitions in Florida for the last six months."

He whistled. "There are a lot of these."

"I know, but if no dogs ran off—or weren't kidnapped in any other past event—it might make it easier to narrow down our suspects."

"Our?"

Darn it. "Your suspects."

The slight tilt of his head and the imperceptible upturn of his lips implied I'd impressed him. "I'll get right on this. Anything else?" he asked.

Wanting to be totally transparent with the law, I let him know my pink aura theory.

"You think this aura might be a spell that lures a dog away from its owner?"

If I had told him I had just met an alien, he would have acted less surprised. I wouldn't be put off though. "It's just a theory."

His lips almost formed a smile. "Good to know."

Since that seemed to be about all the time he was going to give me, I pushed back my chair. "Where's Steve?" I hadn't really meant to ask, but I was eternally curious.

"Doing his job."

Okay. The boys' club was in full force. After chatting with Pearl once more, and sadly learning nothing new, I needed to do one more thing before I could relax. Now that the dog was confirmed missing, I wanted to confer with Gertrude once more about the pink aura and what it could mean. If that failed, I'd pass my theory by Bertha and Hazel to see if they were aware of a spell that could hypnotize a person or animal.

When I entered the Psychics Corner, the lobby had quite a few people, unlike the last time I was there. I walked up to Sarah. "By any chance is Gertrude free? I only need a minute of her time."

Sarah checked her computer screen. "She has an appointment in ten minutes."

"That's perfect." I smiled and dashed off before she told me not to disturb the psychic.

Sarah must think I was a free-loader rushing in all the time. Truth was, I had tried to pay both Jack and Gertrude, but they wouldn't take any money.

I knocked on her door. When she called out for me to come in, I entered.

She let out a breath. "Oh, Glinda. I was about to call you."

That didn't sound good. "What happened?" I hoped she wasn't ill.

Gertrude was sitting on a hard-backed chair next to a loveseat. I figured the non-cushioned chair was easier to get out of than the soft sofa.

Her office was even more cozy than Jack's in part because she had flowers under her window sill and tall lamps on either side of her desk that cast a warm glow in the room.

"I saw another pink aura," she announced. "This time it was around a smaller dog, one with sandy-colored pointed ears."

Another aura. My pulse skyrocketed. "That's not good." I mentally ran through the dogs. My guess would be Snookums, the Papillon. "I think I should call the sheriff and warn him."

"Yes, dear. You do that."

I pulled out my phone, and my hands were shaking too much to even swipe the call button. I forced my heart to slow. When I calmed a bit, I contacted Steve.

"Sheriff Rocker."

He didn't know it was me? It didn't matter. "Sheriff, it's Glinda."

"I'm a bit busy, Glinda. Can it wait?"

"No, it can't. Gertrude, the psychic, had another vision of—"

"Let me guess," he said. "She saw a pink aura around another dog."

Dread pooled in my stomach. "Yes. Don't tell me he's missing too?"

"I'm afraid so."

Chapter Seven

M Y HEART REFUSED to slow down. "Which dog was it?" I asked, despite being rather sure.

"He is a Papillon belonging to..." A paper rustled. "A Patty O'Neal."

"I met her yesterday. That is terrible. Does anyone have any clues as to his location?"

"I'm working on it. I have to go but call again if you learn something."

I really appreciated that he believed I could help. "I will."

I disconnected and turned back to Gertrude. "I guess you heard. A second dog was taken."

"Yes, but neither dog will be harmed," she announced with great calm.

That was good news. Since she had yet to be wrong, I wouldn't ask her how she knew that. "Did you see anything else in your vision besides the pink aura? Like what the person who took the dog looked like?"

"No. Nothing. I wish I did."

Too bad. It would have been super helpful if she had seen where the dogs were being held. "I know you have a client, but I have a quick question. Have you heard of a spell that hypnotizes a person or an animal?"

She sat there so long, I feared she might have suffered a stroke. "Yes and no. There are suggestion spells, but I'm guessing you want to know if any one of them comes with a pink aura?"

Gertrude could read minds. "Yes."

"Not specifically. All of the spells I ever did were for good. I would never hypnotize someone without their consent—dogs included."

This was scary stuff. "Do you think a black witch is involved?" I didn't know of any, but I was sure they existed. There were covens all over Florida.

"Most likely, but please do not look for this person, or you could end up in a very bad place."

Goosebumps ran up and down my body. "Good to know."

Someone knocked on Gertrude's door, and then Sarah poked her head in. "Your next appointment is here."

That was my cue to leave. "Thank you, Gertrude."

"Any time."

It had been a long day, and I needed to unwind. There was a slim chance that Iggy had found out something. Those visiting town didn't have a lot of choices where to eat. Dolly's diner was the closest to the park, but her place only had ten booths. While we only had ten indoor tables, many ate at the bar or on our expansive outdoor patio.

Not wanting any part of the madhouse inside the restaurant, I went through the side entrance and up the stairs where I found Iggy on the sofa instead of on his stool.

"About time you got home," he said.

"If there was a way for me to text or even phone you, I

would have." Sheesh. It wasn't as if he could even use a cell phone. "From the way your tail is moving, you've learned something."

"I have."

"Let me put down my things and grab a drink. I'm parched. A lot has happened today for me too."

Iggy followed me into the kitchen. Either he wanted something to eat too, or he was chomping at the bit to learn or to share. "Tell me," I said as I grabbed a glass from the cupboard.

"Two women who seemed to know the contestants were eating lunch."

That wasn't earth shattering news. "And?"

"They were talking about these two women, Patty and Michelle."

"There is a Patty O'Neal who owns a Papillon. Did you know her dog went missing maybe a half hour ago?" I was making the time up, but it had happened recently.

"No. That makes sense now."

"Sense, how?"

"Apparently, many years ago, Patty stole another woman's husband—a woman by the name of Michelle."

I remember serving Patty, her husband, and her two kids. She seemed nice. "Interesting, but there are a lot of women by the name of Michelle in the world." I checked the list for one. "I see a Michelle Stewart has a dog she entered in the contest. Do you think that could be the same woman?"

"From the way these two women at lunch were gossiping? Absolutely."

That might be something else for Steve to investigate.

Since Patty's dog was missing, it was possible that Michelle had something to do with it. "Did you learn anything about Josh Randall? His dog was taken too."

"No. Got any leaves for me?" Iggy asked.

Apparently, he had given me enough valuable information and wanted his reward. "Sure."

I fixed him a nice plate and even threw in two blueberries. On occasion, he liked those too. I carried the plate to the coffee table and then sat down.

"I think I need a spreadsheet," I announced more to remind myself than to Iggy.

"Is that the answer to all of life's problems?" Iggy asked.

"Maybe. It helps me organize my thoughts."

"I should have one too."

I laughed. "Is your life that complicated?"

He lifted his chest. "Do you know what it's like having a cat for a girlfriend?"

I worked hard not to laugh again. "I can't say that I do."

"She's stuck up and ignores me."

And yet, he still liked her. "Aimee is a cat."

"She doesn't act that way with Aunt Fern," Iggy said.

I had to say Aimee did seem to adore my aunt. "True."

Before our discussion could continue, my cell rang. "I should take this. It might be important."

Iggy turned to the side to see and hear better. The call was from Penny. She'd worked for me today, because she had something to do with her seven-year-old son tomorrow.

"Hey, Penny."

"What are you doing tonight?" she asked.

"Besides resting? Nothing."

"You have to do me a favor."

I was all favored out, but saying no to Penny was impossible. "What is it?"

"Sam and I are going on a date, and I'm petrified."

I chuckled. "Correct me if I'm wrong, but weren't you married to this guy?"

"Yes," she said. "But we broke up two years ago, because well…you know. This will be our first date since the divorce."

Perhaps there was a good reason why they hadn't dated since then. Sam had been into some bad stuff after they married, which was why Penny divorced him. Ever since his former partner in crime had been sentenced to jail time for accessory to murder, Sam had, in theory, cleaned up his act. "You'll be fine. Where are you going?" It wouldn't be romantic if they ate at the Tiki Hut Grill.

"Sam suggested we drive over to Holland. He said there is a rather nice steak place there."

I was impressed. "Steak sounds divine, but be careful. You've told me all the stories about how easy it was for him to charm you. Remember, as soon as you fell for him, he turned on you."

"I know. I called because I want us to double date. Talking with Sam throughout dinner might be a bit much."

Two issues came to mind. One was that I didn't have a second half to this double date, and secondly, if one couldn't sit through a dinner with someone, how were they ever going to be together in the long run? To my credit, I didn't voice either of those issues. Well, I was about to mention the lack of a date, because while I was a witch, love spells weren't my forte.

"Glinda?" Penny asked. "What do you say?"

"Did you have a date for me in mind?"

"I do. Jaxson."

Mixed emotions slammed into me. Did she want to have him on this double date because she wanted him for herself? When Jaxson first came into town a few months back, Penny had been smitten. She'd seemed interested in learning what she'd missed out on all those years ago in high school. Or was she really trying to help me? I wanted to believe the latter.

"You do know we're just friends, right? Jaxson is too valuable a resource to ruin by dating him."

"Fine, then how about Steve?"

That made me laugh. "You might not have heard, but another dog was kidnapped. He's a bit busy."

"I know. I even heard the competition has been canceled. The other entrants are afraid something will happen to their dogs too."

"What?" Why hadn't someone told me? Like Steve. "That is a real shame, but I'd be afraid too."

"I don't blame them either. So, what do you say to double dating?" Penny asked.

While this wasn't a video call, I could almost see her lips turn into a pout. I didn't believe in beating around the bush. "I'm not the type to ask someone out on a date," I announced.

She laughed, all traces of begging gone. "This is the twenty-first century, you know."

"I do, Miss Smarty Pants."

"What about Drake then?" Penny said.

"You know he doesn't date women."

"Okay, you pick. What about the new deputy? I heard

he's hot," Penny said, with a hunk of slyness thrown in for good measure.

Enough was enough. "I'm sure Jaxson is working tonight, since this is their busiest night of the week, but I'll ask him."

"He's free. I heard Trace is working tonight."

When did she suddenly become Miss Gossip? I looked over at Iggy. Penny was talking loud enough for him to be able to listen in. I mouthed, *What should I do?*

He did the little lift-the-foot-thing, indicating a shrug. "I'll see what I can do. Do you want to meet somewhere?"

If we were going to Holland, we should probably meet here and drive together. On the other hand, if the two of them got into a fight, it could become rather awkward. Jaxson and I had been in the car together when we needed to discuss something with Morgan Oliver's aunt, and it had been fine.

"Sure. How about the parking lot next to the Tiki Hut?" she said.

"Works for me. What time?"

"It's about five now. How about six?" she asked.

"Great. See you then."

After I hung up, I wasn't sure I wanted to subject Jaxson to a possibly uncomfortable evening with two people he didn't know well, but Penny wouldn't forgive me if I didn't at least try. Before I lost my nerve, I found Jaxson's number and called it.

"You heard, I take it?" Jaxson asked as a way of a greeting.

"And by hear, I'm guessing you mean there was a second dog kidnapped and the competition was canceled?"

"You knew?" he asked.

His hint of anger was what I always experienced when I

was the last to know. "Penny just called a few seconds ago and told me." I was referring to the show cancellation. I was aware of the dognapping before, but I didn't tell Jaxson, because this wasn't really his case—not that it was mine either.

"Oh."

Before the silence became too awkward, I needed to ask him out. "Penny, the same Penny you went to school with—"

"Penny Carsted. I know her. She works with you."

"Yes. Well, she was married to a guy named Sam."

"I went to school with him too."

Darn. This asking someone out was hard. "Yes, you did. Anyway, they're divorced, but the two of them are now trying to give it a go again. They are having their first real date tonight and asked if we could join them."

More silence.

"Tonight?" he asked.

"Yes, as in one hour." I held my breath.

"Why me?"

Was he kidding? Did he expect me to say I was pining for him? I liked him, sure, but romance spoiled everything. "You know both of them—or at least you did eleven years ago."

He chuckled, and relief washed through me. "I didn't picture you as the scrape-the-bottom-of-the-barrel type of girl, but sure, I'll go."

My protest was on the tip of my tongue about his low opinion of himself, but we could discuss it later. "Fantastic. I'll owe you one. We're meeting them at six in the Tiki Hut parking lot. I'll drive since Sam has picked out a restaurant in Holland. I think he wants to get away from the crowds here."

"Smart. See you there."

I disconnected, not liking how fast my heart was beating. This was just a date of convenience, right? I didn't want to call it a date-date. Or was I fooling myself, as usual?

Since our meeting time was fast approaching, I rushed to my bedroom to shower and change. Considering Sam didn't have a lot of money, I suspected the steak place wouldn't be particularly fancy. Still, I wanted to look nice.

Since all of my clothes were pink, it was only a matter of choosing which top went well with which bottoms. Considering it was summer, the restaurant would probably be freezing. For some reason, the establishments believed all customers liked it cold—all except Aunt Fern, who liked to save money.

After changing a few times, I finally went with dark pink jeans, a pale pink lightweight shirt, and my low-top pink Converse sneakers. If I ever purchased a different color shirt or a pair of conventional blue jeans, it might freak Jaxson out.

For makeup, I put on my usual fare of light pink lipstick, some pink blush, and of course, pink eyeliner.

I stepped into the living room and grabbed my keys, credit card, and phone. "Don't wait up for me," I told Iggy.

"If I'm not here, don't worry," he shot back.

I spun around. "Where are you going to be?"

"Aunt Fern loves it when I keep her and Uncle Harold company."

"I bet she does. I think that is great." In reality, Iggy was probably just trying to get into Aimee's good graces.

At five minutes to six, I headed downstairs. Aunt Fern must have been in her apartment, because Bertie Sidwell was at the cash register. Good. I didn't have time to chat anyway. I merely waved and rushed outside. To my delight, Jaxson was already waiting for me.

I slowed as I took a double take. His black jeans hugged his body quite nicely, and the white button-down shirt was tailored to show off his buff body. The polished boots were a nice touch too. I couldn't help but wonder if he thought of this as a date. He'd never shown any interest in me, but I was never really good at reading those kind of signals.

"Hey," I said. "You look nice."

As soon as the words were out of my mouth, I wasn't sure if I should have said them. Then Penny's words came back to me about this being the twenty-first century.

He smiled, but I refused to swoon. We worked together for goodness sake.

"I like your outfit too," he shot back.

"Thanks." I spotted Penny and Sam coming toward us.

Her skin tight dress, high heels, and dramatic makeup implied I probably should have asked for the dress code. It was too late now. Even Sam, who I had never seen in anything other than ratty jeans and a T-shirt had dressed in dark jeans and a nice shirt.

Penny rushed up to me. "This is so exciting. I can't remember the last time we double-dated."

"I can. Never." I said.

She laughed, but it came out rather nervous. "Silly me. Ready?"

"Yes, but if you don't mind, let's take separate cars." I let her decode what I meant.

"Sure, whatever," Penny said.

"Where exactly is this restaurant?" I asked.

Sam handed Jaxson a piece of paper. I was guessing it had

an address on it. Jaxson studied it. "It should be easy to find. See you guys there."

As I walked to my car, Jaxson stepped next to me and held out his hand. "I'll drive."

"I'm perfectly capable. It was my car. It didn't matter he'd insisted the last time."

"I didn't say you weren't. I'm a guy. Guys drive."

I wasn't in the mood to fight testosterone, so I dropped my car keys in his palm and then climbed into the passenger seat.

This was definitely going to be an interesting evening.

Chapter Eight

I TOLD MYSELF this wasn't a real date, but it sure felt like it. It didn't matter that I had asked Jaxson to join me and not the other way around. I still found it rather odd that Penny was uncomfortable being alone with Sam. My question was why go out then? But that was Penny. Or, was she using that as an excuse to get the two of us together? Penny was a romantic, so perhaps that had been her ploy all along.

The problem I faced at the moment was that Jaxson seemed excited about the evening, and that was something I never would have expected. Me? I tried not to think about it much, as those kind of thoughts always fogged the brain. I had to admit he smelled good, and his wet hair looked sexy, and I couldn't forget those polished boots. Who did that unless they wanted to impress a date?

What was I feeling? I'm not sure. I had never discussed my real feelings about him to Aunt Fern or to Penny, but if say Gertrude Pool—who I was sure was not a gossip—would have asked me what I thought about Jaxson Harrison, I'd say I was confused.

A month ago, I might have said that I liked Steve Rocker. He was new in town, good looking, smart, and kind. Sure, he thought I was a bit crazy, but after I helped solve his robbery case at Floyd Paxton's house, he started to believe in my talents.

Jaxson was six years older than me, but I had known him most of my life. Before he served his prison time, he was trouble. Even Drake said he was. As teenagers, Drake and I didn't discuss our families much, so I never learned why Jaxson acted out.

Eleven years went by without a Jaxson sighting, and to be honest, I didn't think about him. When he returned to Witch's Cove, he was understandably angry since he'd been falsely accused of a crime. As soon as his record was cleared though, he changed for the better.

He looked over at me and smiled. "Why so quiet?" he asked.

Whoops! "Just thinking."

"About?"

I wasn't about to say him. "About the dogs."

"You are tenacious, I'll give you that. Have you learned anything new?"

"I have." I filled Jaxson in on the recent developments, including Iggy's information about the two women, Michelle and Patty, and how they might have it in for each other. While he listened intently, I realized I should have told him the truth. "I kind of lied before."

He glanced over at me. "About what?"

"I wasn't thinking about the case. I was thinking about you."

His grin said it all. He liked me, or so I thought. My first instinct was to withdraw, but even I knew that wasn't healthy.

"Is that so? Good or bad?"

I couldn't be totally honest. "We've worked together on Morgan's case and now this one, but I don't know all that much about you."

His forehead furrowed. "Sure, you do. You know I got into trouble in high school, was accused of a crime I didn't commit, spent time in jail, went back to school, and then moved here."

"Those are facts."

"And?" he asked.

I rarely probed into someone's personal life—I did have my limits—but I wanted to know about Jaxson—about the loves of his life, his dreams, and his hopes. But those topics were too personal, at least this soon in our friendship. "I guess I'd like to know the real Jaxson Harrison."

He laughed. "What you see is what you get, sweetheart."

"But you're so different now."

He glanced over at me. "I grew up."

That seemed like a safe topic to pursue. "Okay, when you were young, why were you so rebellious? Drake wasn't."

"Ah, the age-old question. How can parents raise two such different kids?"

"I'm an only child, so I have nothing to compare it to," I said.

"I think Drake is the way he is because of me."

That was a bit cryptic. "Like you raised him or something?"

Jaxson laughed. "No. I didn't do well in school on purpose, and as a result, I was always getting into trouble. Because of that, Dad gave me a lot of unwanted attention. Drake saw that and decided he wouldn't follow in my footsteps."

"I can see Drake doing that."

He flashed me a smile. "Good."

That still didn't answer the *why*. "Why go the bad route instead of the good?"

"Ah, the ever-curious Glinda. We have about twenty more minutes to this drive, and you won't let me alone until I answer, right?"

I lightly punched him in the arm. "I'm not that bad."

"Yes, you are."

Okay, I was. "Fine. Why be bad?"

He blew out a breath. "I've done a lot of thinking about that. In prison, all you have is time to think."

I liked where this was headed. Jaxson never seemed the deep thinker type, but now I believe I'd misjudged him. "Go on."

"Dad was a hard worker. In fact, all he did was work. It was rare for him to find the time to throw a baseball to me or take me on any kind of adventure. The only way for him to even notice me was if I acted out. Dad believed in education more than anything."

I could fill in the blanks. "If you did poorly in school, he'd have to do something about it."

"Exactly." He pressed his lips together for a moment. "I was good in math. So good in fact, that I knew how to mess up on a test and make it look like I didn't know what I was doing. Dad loved math too, so he would tutor me on weekends."

"You enjoyed that, didn't you?" I never would have expected the tough as nails jock to be so needy. Ever.

"I did."

"Did you ever tell him what you did?" I asked.

He chuckled. "Are you kidding? I'm still afraid of what he might do or say."

I'm sure that wasn't true, but it was a sweet sentiment. "Thank you," I said.

"For?"

"For sharing."

He squeezed my leg. "That's because I expect the same back."

Uh-oh. "How about them Tampa Bay Bucs?"

"What?"

I laughed. "That's a football reference to one of Florida's teams."

"I know who they are." He tapped the wheel. "Ah. I get it. That's your avoidance phrase. You never were good dealing with your feelings."

What? "How would you know?" It didn't matter if it was the truth or not.

"Drake and I have talked about you once or twice."

I didn't want to ask about that. "Good to know."

"Tell me why you are so afraid?"

I hope he wasn't talking about emotional fear. Even I didn't understand it, but I had my theories. "I'll tell you this much, and then we need to discuss a safer topic."

He laughed. "Fine."

"My father is a funeral director. He is kind, gentle, and open to everyone he talks with. But when it comes to his own daughter though, he doesn't know how to act."

"I get it. To avoid being hurt, you withdraw. You smile, ask about others because it is safer, and try to be the best you can."

I was stunned. "Yes."

"Fair enough. You don't like talking about yourself. I'll respect that. I have a lot of topics I don't want to discuss either. Tell me more about the dog investigation."

I'd already mentioned that two of the contestants might have had it in for each other. "I'm hoping that Steve can look into past events and see if any dogs had disappeared," I said. "That might help point a finger at someone if there is any overlap in contestants."

"That sounds good. If the thief is someone local, do you have anyone in mind for the dognapping?" he asked. He almost sounded happy we were no longer discussing our feelings.

"Not really, though I think we need to find out more about the entrants. If Michelle and Patty have a history, who's to say others don't?"

"True. It's like anything that involves a common ground, whether you are in law enforcement, a lawyer, an eye doctor, or a dog trainer. Go to enough events and you are bound to run into the same people over and over again," he said.

"That is an interesting point. I need to create a spreadsheet about who might be guilty. I'll focus on the relationships between the contestants. There are very few people in this world who have no secrets."

He glanced over at me before returning his gaze to the road. "Ain't that the truth."

I said nothing for a bit, remembering Jaxson as a much younger man. I'd met his dad many times and could see now why he turned out the way he did.

As Aunt Fern would say: The past is in the past and should be left there. While I thought it was a dumb comment at the time, it applied here. That meant I had to focus on the present—which was getting us to the restaurant.

Since Jaxson was driving, it was my job to navigate. "It should be about a mile up the road on the right."

"Roger that."

We arrived just as Penny and Sam were getting out of their car. Jaxson adeptly parallel parked in front of the restaurant, a talent I had never fully developed.

Not wanting to test whether he planned to open the door for me, I pushed it open myself. Instead of looking over at him for his reaction to our rather intimate conversation, I focused on the steakhouse. It looked quite fancy with its large wooden door. The windows were made with wavy glass, and the carriage lamps on the outside gave off an air of sophistication. Overall, it had a German feel to it.

I was the first to admit that I didn't expect something this nice. Go Sam. Penny had said he'd recently changed jobs—it must be one that paid better.

Sam reached the door first and held it open for us. "Thank you, Sam," I said.

He smiled. The man was smart to know that if he could impress me, it would make it easier for Penny to agree to be with him. For the sake of their child, I hoped things worked out, despite their tumultuous history.

Once we were seated, we each picked up the menus, pretending it was the most interesting thing in the world. I was seated next to Jaxson, but I couldn't think about that anymore.

Penny might be my best friend, but I wasn't sure what to talk about either. The last time Sam and I had interacted, it was right after I took potentially incriminating evidence of a crime I thought Sam might have committed to Sheriff Rocker. Thankfully, Sam had been innocent. I internally laughed. That was one thing Sam and Jaxson had in common. Some people from Witch's Cove believed they were both criminals, and it turned out both had been innocent.

"I heard you're working on a caper," Sam said, breaking the ice.

A caper? That word reminded me of days of old. "Two dogs from the dog show have gone missing. I wouldn't be involved if one of the psychics hadn't come to me and asked for my help." Truth was, Gertrude hadn't come out and asked me to help, since at the time no dog had been taken. But she had implied it.

"I'm sure you'll get to the bottom of it," Sam said with great confidence.

I supposed his belief in me was slightly well-founded since I had proven he wasn't a murderer.

Before I could elaborate, the front door of the restaurant opened, and who should walk in but none other than Nash Solano and Amy Jones—the owner of the Sheltie named Stumpy. Jaxson had shown me a picture of her when he was doing his research.

My pulse jackknifed. I lifted the menu in front of my face so he wouldn't see me.

Jaxson placed a hand on my arm. "What's wrong?"

"The new deputy is here with one of the contestants."

"Why is that a problem?" Thankfully, Jaxson kept his

voice low.

"Let them sit down first, and then I'll tell you."

The next minute was a bit hairy, but I was pleased when the hostess seated them far enough away so they couldn't hear us. The bad news was that if Nash looked in our direction, he'd see me.

"Glinda, what's wrong?" Penny asked.

"Switch seats with me? Or rather with us. Please."

"Why?" she asked.

"Our new deputy just walked in, and I don't want him to see me."

Penny's mouth opened. "Nash Solano is here?"

Isn't that what I'd just said? "Yes, he's here. Now, get up but don't be obvious. We have to do it without attracting notice."

"How can we do that?"

I felt as if I was in some kind of slap-stick movie. "You go to the bathroom, and then I'll move over to your spot. A minute later, Jaxson can then get up, and Sam will take his place," I said.

"Okay," she whispered. "Excuse me," Penny said in a too-loud voice. She stood and then walked toward the ladies' room.

Pretending I needed to tell Sam something, I moved next to him. After another fake bathroom trip by Jaxson, we were finally sitting where Penny and Sam had been.

"Now tell me what's going on," Penny said, thankfully keeping her voice low.

"The woman with him is one of the dog show contestants."

"I knew it. There is something going on with him. There's been a lot of secrecy surrounding Nash Solano from the moment he entered our town," Penny said.

"I know. Even Jaxson couldn't find much on him."

Penny's eyes widened. "You researched him?"

I couldn't tell if Penny thought that was horrible idea or a great one.

"I did," Jaxson stated.

"Because I asked him to," I said. "The point is that Nash is with Amy. Does that mean he had something to do with the missing dogs? I mean he comes to town and the next day the theft occurs."

Sam held up a hand. "Let's not jump to conclusions—and that is a real stretch. I know what that can do to a person."

He was right. "Give me a reason why they'd be together this far from town."

Jaxson held up a finger. "There aren't a lot of places to eat in Witch's Cove. Even more so now, with the competition in town."

"You have a point."

"I did have the chance to look into Amy. She works here in Holland as an elementary school teacher."

"Oh. Do you think Nash interviewed her, and because he thought she was hot, he asked her out?" Not that they'd know the answer, but I wanted their opinion.

Jaxson let out a breath. "I didn't think you were the conspiratorial type, Glinda."

Ouch. "I'm not. At least not usually. I just like to understand what we're dealing with."

Penny leaned forward. "If Amy teaches here, she's practically a Witch's Cove local. I'm betting Maude or Miriam would have the scoop on her."

"You're probably right."

Jaxson leaned back. "Now that we have that settled, let's enjoy ourselves."

He was right. I'd become too consumed with this case, so much so that not only had I forgotten my father's fiftieth birthday, I'd forgotten that I was supposed to bake a few dishes. That was wrong on so many levels. Tomorrow after work, I'd shop and then cook. I didn't have the time to go driving around town looking for the dogs.

That wouldn't be a big deal since I was rather confident that Jaxson would probably do his computer magic. Unless I found out something concrete to offer the sheriff, my job was done.

Just realizing that helped relax me. When the server came over to take our order, I asked for a glass of Chardonnay and a nice juicy steak. I was ready to enjoy the company.

Chapter Nine

"HOW WAS YOUR date?" Iggy asked as he waddled into the kitchen early the next morning.

"Fine."

"Fine? That's not an answer. I want to know if you enjoyed yourself."

Who was he? "You sound like Mom or Aunt Fern."

Iggy opened and then shut his mouth. "That's because I care about you."

I chuckled. "It's because you are nosy."

He lifted his head. "That too."

Knowing Iggy, if I didn't give him some news, he'd push. I thought about telling him that Nash and Amy were at the restaurant, but I feared my pink blabbermouth might tell the wrong person. "I had a very nice time. I even enjoyed being with adults instead of listening to gossip and following clues."

"Cool."

That was it? Just cool? I doubt he'd let it drop, but I hoped he did.

"I thought so."

"What are you doing now?" Iggy asked as he waddled closer and then crawled up the side of the counter to the counter top. I swear, there was no place he couldn't reach.

"After work, I need to make my cranberry sauce as well as a sweet potato casserole for Dad's birthday tomorrow. But before that, I have to stop by the store to buy the ingredients."

I had very few supplies since most of my meals were cooked by the restaurant chef.

"You know how to cook?" Iggy asked.

I glanced over at him. "Funny, funny. Just because I don't do it often, doesn't mean I don't know how." He'd seen me prepare meals before.

He lifted his head higher. "Who's going to the party?"

I had to remember what my mother told me. "Besides Aunt Fern, I think Tim and Sheila Oglethorpe. Those are their best friends."

"Don't they own the flower shop?" he asked.

I was impressed that Iggy paid attention to such things. "They do. You have a good memory."

He puffed out his chest with pride. "I do, don't I?"

"Yes, you do."

"What about your uncles? Are they coming?"

That was a sore spot. "I don't think so. Dad's family now lives out of state."

"It's a big birthday. When you turned twenty-one, you had a big blow out bash."

"That's true." I was still in college, and all of my friends had thrown a surprise party for me. Some of the events from that night might never be remembered.

"Are you asking Jaxson to your dad's party?" Iggy asked.

Why in the world did he think I would? "No. I doubt he'd enjoy himself. I'm not sure he even remembers my dad, who I love by the way, but he's rather…"

"Stuffy and Beta?"

I was shocked. "Iggy Goodall. That's not a nice thing to say."

"It's true, you know."

My familiar had a point, though I was surprised he was even aware of the difference between an Alpha male and a Beta one. "Being Beta isn't a bad thing, you know. Dad is a funeral director. He has to exude sympathy and kindness." I just wished he'd been more open with me growing up.

"You need a bad boy to counteract your stubbornness."

I laughed, because what he said might be true. Jaxson certainly had been a bad boy, but the problem was that I still liked Steve. He wasn't a bad boy in the traditional sense. His determination to do the right thing appealed to me. Either that, or I had a need to prove to him I wasn't a quack.

"What do you know about relationships?" I asked as I fixed a bowl of cereal. I couldn't spend too long chatting. I had to get to work.

"Ouch. I'd like to see you handle a cat."

Now I'd offended him. "I meant human relationships."

"I know more than you think. I'm a keen observer of human behavior," he said.

He might be right. "I'd be happy to discuss my love life further, but my shifts starts in a few minutes."

Once I finished my quick meal, I donned the rest of my costume and headed downstairs, ready to tackle what I suspected would be a busy day.

AFTER A NEVER-ENDING eight hours, I headed upstairs. Iggy was in the kitchen, clearly waiting to be fed. "Let me change, and I'll fix you a plate of greens."

"Okay."

Once I took off my costume, I pulled on a pair of baggy pants and a loose top. I then fixed Iggy his greens and placed a bowl of water on the floor.

"I need a few things from the store," I told him. "I'll be back in a jiff."

"Okay. Take your time," he said.

"You aren't going to do anything, are you?"

He looked up at me. "No."

I had the sense that Iggy would always be trouble.

True to my word, I drove to the store, bought the few necessary ingredients, and returned home in under forty-five minutes. I was happy the store was fairly empty, because it allowed me to zip in and out.

"I'm home," I called as I entered. I tossed the keys on the side table and stepped into the kitchen.

Iggy was there still enjoying his food. "What are you getting your dad for his birthday?" he asked. "A whoopie cushion?"

Who had raised this animal? It had to be Aunt Fern's influence. "No. A tie and some cufflinks."

"Bor-ing."

"Then he should think it's the perfect gift."

Iggy lifted a claw, but I was too preoccupied to figure out what he meant. I was sure it wasn't a nice gesture.

Focus. I located a small saucepan and placed it on the stove. After setting out the dried cranberries, the cranberry juice, some sugar, and the salt shaker on the counter, I was ready to go.

I didn't need to check the recipe since every time the family got together, I was asked to make the same two dishes. Last Christmas, I wanted to be adventurous and try my hand at a spinach quiche. I had forgotten to pick up heavy cream, and the half and half replacement I had in the fridge made the quiche watery. After that fiasco, I was relegated to the two things I was good at making.

I placed the ingredients into the pot and turned on the heat. It wasn't long before the liquid boiled. Once I mixed the cornstarch and water together, I slowly poured it into the mixture, making sure to stir the pot in between each addition. When it came to a boil again, I took it off the stove to cool.

"You need to grow a hibiscus plant so you can feed me the flowers," Iggy announced without prompting.

I laughed, partly because I didn't know where that comment came from. "I have a black thumb, which is why I don't have any plants in my apartment."

"You're just saying that, so you don't have to take the time to water the plant."

"I'd kill it for sure. Maybe Aunt Fern would have better luck." Or wasn't this about the plant, but rather about me caring for him?

Jaxson had acted out because his father had been too busy to pay attention to him. I hoped I wasn't doing the same thing to Iggy.

He climbed down from the counter, clearly bored with my cooking. "I'll ask her."

"I think she is working," I called after him.

The cat door swung open. Oh, my. How had I managed to raise such an entitled animal? Or was it a cry for help?

Before I put the cranberries into the blender, I started the yam casserole. I didn't know what the calorie count was for even a half of a cup of this recipe, but I bet it was high. Since Dad seemed to be losing weight at an alarming rate, I wanted to make the recipe as rich as possible. That meant real brown sugar and pure butter. It was the raisins and mini marshmallows on top that really was the *pièce de résistance*.

After I blended the cranberries and stored the final product in the refrigerator, I finished making the yams. Since I wouldn't be serving them until tomorrow, I didn't have to heat them until then.

Once I was done, I poured myself a glass of wine and dropped onto the sofa, wondering how my life seemed to have gotten so out of control.

Chapter Ten

IT WAS ONLY five, yet I was feeling a bit unsettled. It was Sunday, which meant the very ancient theater in town would be showing some classic movie. I hadn't been there in probably a year, but I thought it would do me good to get out. This whole mystery of the pink aura was stressing me out, and I needed a break to clear my head.

One thing I loved about that place was that the building had been erected in the 1920s yet still maintained its charm. The ceiling was painted a bright blue, with luminescent stars placed in no particular order, and the interior was made to look like a Broadway theater right down to the painted box seats that only looked real when the lights were low. It even had a mezzanine section. In front of the movie screen was a stage. When I was little, before the show began, an organ and its accompanist would rise from below and play a song or two. Oh, how I used to look forward to going with my parents.

I checked out the movie schedule to see which movie was showing. When I saw the title, I squealed.

Iggy jerked to attention. "What happened?"

"They're playing *Murder On The Orient Express* at the theater—the 1974 version, not the newer one."

"Oh. I thought maybe the new *Star Wars* movie was out."

They were still making those? "No, this is a classic."

"Haven't you seen it like ten times?" Iggy asked.

"Yes, but each time I watch the movie, I see something I missed."

I snapped my fingers. The Howl At The Moon Emporium was closed today. Maybe Drake wanted to go. He was a classic movie buff too. I dialed his number.

"Hey, I heard you had an interesting evening last night," Drake said as a way of a greeting.

"I did." I hadn't thought Jaxson would say anything. It wasn't as if we'd kissed goodnight or anything. We'd started as friends and ended as friends. Since I didn't want Drake to ask any more questions—ones I wasn't ready to answer, I continued. "*Murder On The Orient Express* is playing at the theater tonight. Do you want to go? It will be like old times."

"Sunday nights at that theater brings back a lot of memories."

"It does, doesn't it?" He didn't need to say that after Jaxson had been arrested, our lives had also changed, and we rarely ever went. "Are you interested in going?"

"Sure, but you already know the ending of the movie."

"Because I've seen it a bunch of times?"

"Of course," he said.

"That's the fun of it. I like to find things I haven't noticed before."

"You amaze me, Glinda Goodall," Drake said.

His comment was warm and comfortable. "Show starts at six thirty. Meet you there?"

"How about l pick you up at six? I know we could walk, but I don't want to get all sticky before the show."

That was something I would say. "Perfect."

I knew this wasn't a date. Drake always implied he wasn't into women, but I'd never seen him with a man either. He was reliable, a good listener, and hot. I never understood why he wasn't married with kids—regardless of who his partner was.

Right now, I wanted to take a shower, grab a quick bite, and then change.

At six on the dot, I was outside waiting for my ride. I had asked Iggy to go with us, but he said the movie was boring. I couldn't blame him. This version was made a long time ago, but no one was as amazing as Agatha Christie.

Drake's car pulled into the lot, and I was surprised to find Jaxson was with him. I slid in the back.

"I hope you don't mind if my brother joins us," Drake said as he pulled onto the road.

"Of course not. The more the merrier." I meant it too. Did my face flush from inhaling Jaxson's cologne? Maybe. But tonight, I was determined to relax. Or was I in denial?

I would have said this was like old times, except I don't think the three of us ever went out together. "I didn't know you liked old movies, Jaxson."

He glanced in the rearview mirror. "I am a man of mystery and many talents."

I laughed, as I'm sure was his intention. One of those talents, however, was probably not enjoying old Agatha Christie movies.

No surprise, the parking lot was mostly empty. Even though I could hear Jaxson saying that a man should pay for a woman, because he'd picked up the tab for our steak dinner, I pulled out my credit card first. "My treat, since I invited you." Actually, I only invited Drake, but it didn't matter.

Drake grinned. "Great. I love it. I wish there were more people like you."

He was teasing, but I appreciated that he didn't want me to be embarrassed.

With our tickets in hand, we stepped into the theater where history surrounded me again.

"Let's sit upstairs," Jaxson suggested.

"Why?" I loved it up there, but I was curious to know Jaxson's reasoning.

"I like being able to see everyone."

I laughed. "At this moment, we are the only ones in the theater." The rest were still in the lobby at the concession stand.

"So?" he asked.

Both of the Harrison boys seemed to be enjoying this. To be honest, so was I. After a few previews of coming movies, the old movie began, and I sat back to dissect every sentence.

Throughout the movie, I was struck by the amazing mind of Hercule Poirot. I remained in awe of his logic, his unemotional analysis of the case, and his ability to see through a person's lies. I was nothing like this man. I believed what most people told me—so unlike Hercule. I never understood where the math side of my brain went when I worked on a case, since I often let emotion get the best of me.

Since Drake had seen the movie many times too, he'd throw out a spoiler every now and then about how that person was related to the little girl who'd been abducted years before.

When the show finished, we headed out. "That was

great," I said. "Thanks for joining me."

"Our pleasure," Drake said. "I figured you'd want to go because rumor has it someone is interested in tearing down this building and the ice cream shop next door to put up a condominium.

My heart dropped to my stomach. "No! They can't do that. The theater has been around since Methuselah."

"That's the point. I wouldn't be surprised if the rafters are full of termites, and this place needs to come down," Drake said.

"Way to be a downer."

Jaxson placed a hand on my back and steered me left instead of to the car. "That's why we need to have an ice cream sundae at the shop. I grew up here too, remember?"

These two were good to me. "You twisted my arm."

The inside was rather crowded—unlike the theater—but we managed to snag a table. I sighed. "Drake, how many hours did we spend in this place during high school?" I asked. Yes, I sounded a bit sad, but that was because the memories came flooding back.

The place was as tacky as it had been all those years ago, but I loved the metal tables and the uncomfortable seats with the red leather cushions. The lights were bright—actually too bright—but that was part of its charm. It was loud, too, filled mostly with the younger crowd who wasn't old enough to go to a bar. I had to say, being here was better than any drinking establishment for my mental state right now.

"Penny for your thoughts?" Jaxson asked.

"When did you become the sensitive one?" As soon as those words left my mouth, I regretted them. "Strike that. I appreciate that you care enough to ask. I'm a bit sad. I think I wanted to return to Witch's Cove in part because I thought this town would never change."

"Everything changes," Drake said.

"I know, which is why I want to enjoy it while I can."

Jaxson smiled. "Then let's order and get to the enjoyment part."

The server came over, and we told her what we wanted. "How did you hear they might tear down this place?" I asked Drake.

"Oh, no you don't. We are not talking about it. I never should have mentioned it."

"What Drake means, is that if you know who the developer is that you'd knock on his door, pleading with him to change his mind."

I blew out a breath and placed my palms on the cool table top. "You are right. I have to stop butting into everyone's affairs."

The two men looked at each other. "Let's not get carried away, Glinda," Jaxson said. "We need people like you to keep everyone honest."

"Thank you."

Once our wonderful desserts were served, I was in heaven. Sweets always soothed my soul. I looked around, trying to memorize the posters on the walls right down to the scuffs on the floor. It would be a real shame to lose something this iconic in town.

Chapter Eleven

THAT NIGHT, I had a bit of trouble sleeping, since I kept thinking about someone wanting to destroy two of my favorite historical sites—historical in that it reminded me of my childhood. I didn't know who was behind it nor was I about to ask. I had enough on my plate. I know, I know, when did that ever stop me before? But this time, I had to control myself. I needed life to get back to normal.

The dog show had been canceled, which meant most of the visitors had left town. The Tiki Hut was once again calm. Of my five assigned tables this morning, only two were occupied.

I had just served them their meals, giving me a moment to chat with Aunt Fern. After the movies and my ice cream shop date, I'd stopped over at her place and asked her if she'd heard about the potential condo project. She had not, which gave me hope that Drake's information might not have been accurate.

After checking to see whether Aimee was with Aunt Fern—she was not—I brought up the birthday party. "What are you taking to Dad's party tonight?" I asked.

"A ham and some mashed potatoes."

My mouth watered. "Yum."

Aunt Fern wagged a finger at me. "I know you. Every time you start with small talk, something is on your mind. Tell me."

My aunt could always read me. "On Saturday, Penny and Sam asked me to double date with them."

"You told me. Jaxson agreed to go with you."

"Yes, but what I didn't say was that I saw Nash Solano at the restaurant in Holland with none other than Amy Jones."

She glanced to the side. "Amy Jones. That name sounds familiar." My aunt returned her focus to me. "Is she one of the dog owners?"

"Yes." I waited for the reality to sink in.

"Why would Deputy Solano be with her?" She leaned her elbows on the counter. "Do you think the two of them were plotting the dog's theft? Is that why he suddenly showed up in town?"

Did I mention I loved my aunt? I swear our minds often worked alike. "That's what I want to know."

"And you waited to tell me this now, why?" She stood erect again.

I hadn't really meant to withhold the information. "I needed time to decide if it was important. Maybe Nash thought she was pretty and asked her out. To avoid prying eyes, they ate at a restaurant in her hometown."

"That makes sense, but from the way you described him, he seems like the cautious type—too cautious in fact to chance being seen with a possible dognapping suspect."

"Exactly. Which means there could be something going on," I said. Or was my imagination getting the best of me, like it often did?

"You know what I would do?"

"Please. Tell me." I respected her opinion.

"Mention it to Steve. See if he thinks it's on the up and up."

I inhaled. "I'll look like a gossip."

She tucked her chin and looked over the rim of her glasses. "What's wrong with being a gossip? We provide valuable input to this community."

That made me laugh. "Okay, Aunt Fern. I'll think about it." That was code for: I'll get Penny's take on this.

When someone new sat down at one of my tables, I went back to work. At around two, the restaurant was virtually empty again, so I pulled Penny aside. "Now that we've had a day to think about it, do you think Nash being with Amy, the dog owner, is cause for concern?"

"Are you kidding? Of course, I do. You need to mention it to Steve. I imagine he won't visibly react but let him decide whether to investigate."

I was hoping she'd say that. "You don't think he'll think of me as just a snoop?"

Penny laughed. "Well, if the shoe fits."

"Ha, ha. Too bad you're right. After work, I'll go over and ask him something innocent. If I don't see Nash, I might bring it up."

She smiled. "You can't let anything go, can you?"

"No, I can't."

For the rest of the afternoon, while I waited on tables, I prepared what I was going to say to Steve. The two dogs were still missing, which was why the decision to cancel the show had been smart. I imagined that Eleanor Aldrich would lose money, but that was better than having another dog disappear. I imagine Nash would check out the list of other venues I'd given him to see if this kind of thing had happened before—assuming he wasn't involved in any of his.

Once my shift finished, I changed and headed over to the sheriff's department. Just my luck, Nash was at his seat working away at his computer, which would make talking about him to Steve a bit difficult.

Jennifer was working instead of Pearl, which I decided might be a good thing. There would be less gossip about why I was always there. "Is the sheriff in?" I asked as politely as I could.

"He is. What is this about?"

I didn't care to announce I wanted to find out about Nash or what he was doing to find the dogs. "It's of a *personal* nature." I smiled sweetly.

Jennifer was married with kids, so I was pretty sure she wasn't interested in him. "I'll let the sheriff know."

"Thanks."

She called him. "He'll see you now," Jennifer said.

It was ridiculous that I was nervous. I liked Nash—what little I knew of him—yet here I was about to tattle on him. I was hoping there was nothing going on between him and Amy that involved the dogs. For starters, it would make the mayor and his hiring team look bad.

I knocked on Steve's door and entered. I was happy Nash was so focused on what he was doing that he didn't seem to notice my arrival.

Steve looked up. "Glinda. Nice to see you again. How can I help you?"

His tone was very professional. Good. I would be just as clinical. "I'm sure this is nothing, but I felt it was my duty to mention that while out to dinner on Saturday in Holland, Nash came into the restaurant with Amy Jones." Darn. That hadn't been subtle at all.

I had actually planned on asking him something more innocent, such as did he know that Miriam and Maude Daniels were having their annual anniversary party of their store opening and if he was invited? But what did I do? I blurted my question about Nash.

I had to assume that Steve was well aware who Amy Jones was. His lips pressed together, and then he leaned back in his chair, twirling the pencil he was holding over his knuckles. "This is a concern of yours why?"

It wasn't, but I wouldn't admit that. "It only is if maybe Nash and Amy colluded to steal the dogs."

He dipped his head. "Steal the dogs. And why would they do that?" he asked. The glint that used to be in his eyes whenever I asked an amusing question returned, implying he liked teasing me.

"I'm not sure. Maybe to sell them on the black market? Amy has been to a lot of these competitions and might have been approached a time or two about selling her dog."

"Interesting. Do you have any evidence to back this up?" One side of his lips quirked up.

He knew I didn't. "No."

"Sit down, Glinda."

Uh-oh. I did. "Do you know something?" I asked, hoping he had a clue as to where the dogs might be.

"I do."

I expected him to continue, but he seemed to want to make me beg. "What is it?"

"Nash told me all about his *date* with Amy. She contacted him because they used to know each other in Montana. But that is neither here nor there. When Amy moved down to Holland, she met Josh Randall."

"Josh? Yuk." He was the stuffy one who owned Mittens.

"They dated for a bit, but his ego was a bit too much for her, so she dumped him."

I had to smile. "I can see why. The man seems really pompous."

"That may be, but Amy feared that Josh would accuse her of trying to get back at him by taking his dog. She wanted to tell Nash before the accusations flew."

"That was smart on her part, but isn't it kind of backward?" I asked.

"How so?"

"If she dumped him, he'd be the one who was mad. He should want to get back at her by taking her dog. Not the other way around."

Steve seemed to think about it for a bit. "Your logic is sound, but regardless, Amy was with Nash to welcome him to Florida and to be up front with him about Josh."

I mulled that over. "I guess nothing underhanded was going on then," I said. Now who felt like a fool? Ah, that would be me.

"Nothing, but thanks for stopping in." I stood. "And Glinda?"

"Yes?"

"Just so you are in the loop, even though the competition

has been canceled, I've asked those directly involved in the competition to stay around for a few days until we find the dogs. It would make my life easier if you didn't butt in."

Butt in? That wasn't a nice thing to say. "If I hadn't butted in with Cliff Duncan's murder or with Morgan Oliver's, those cases might have gone in a different direction."

He held up his hand. "I know, but if you snoop around, someone might decide to take you instead of another dog."

It had occurred to me that I might be putting myself in danger if I asked too many questions, but I planned to be careful. "I promise I won't talk to any of the contestants."

"Thank you."

That didn't mean I wouldn't talk to say one of the Daniel sisters or to Dolly Andrews to find out what they knew. "Did Nash learn whether any dogs had been taken at any of the other events?"

"In fact, he did find out a few things. We are cross referencing whether any of the contestants were at any of those events. That doesn't mean any of them were involved, but maybe a pattern will emerge."

"That sounds good." I appreciated that at least they took my suggestion seriously. I would have asked Steve to let me know if he learned anything, but I needed to stay out of it.

Tonight was my dad's birthday party and then on Wednesday, Maude and Miriam were hosting their annual store opening anniversary party at their coffee shop, which would then move to the tea shop. Apparently, this dual store party had become quite a time-honored tradition in Witch's Cove. "I forgot that I came here in the first place to let you know about the annual Maude and Miriam Daniels' party on

Wednesday. They celebrate the opening of their stores every year."

"I had heard about it. Remember, I have Pearl. I plan to be there."

"Good."

I really wanted to ask who his number one suspect was in this missing dogs' case, but I was sure he wouldn't tell me. And that would be smart of him.

Not wanting to overstay my visit more than I already had, I left. Even though the show had been canceled, I wanted to take another look around the park. There might be some indication a witch was involved in the two abductions—assuming the dogs hadn't run off.

The sun was out, allowing me to enjoy the late afternoon. I wasn't sure what I was looking for, but I kept my eyes peeled. As I toured the far side of the park, I shook my head at the tire tracks on the muddy grass. Someone had driven off the road and across the sidewalk, presumably to park. Sheesh. I was about to ignore it, when the sun hit the ground at the right angle to show some dog prints in the tire tracks. My imagination went wild. I was no expert when it came to dogs, but the paw prints could have belonged to Mittens.

I pulled out my phone. I squatted down and took a few photos of the tire markings and the paw prints. As I stood up, I spotted some white and black hairs sticking out of the mud. My heart raced.

I needed an evidence bag. Even though I didn't think I could leave fingerprints on a strand of hair, I didn't want Steve to be upset if I messed up the case. Before I touched the few tuffs, I took the best picture I could. Unfortunately, the quality of the photo didn't show as much detail as I'd hoped.

I glanced around. The best I could do was use a leaf to pick up the few strands. With the evidence in hand, I hurried back to the department. I barged in. "I need an evidence bag," I told Jennifer.

Her brows furrowed. "For a leaf?"

I blew out a breath. Before I could explain, Nash came over. "What do you have?"

I explained about the tire tracks, the paw prints, and the tuffs of hair.

He smiled. "We saw them too—the tire tracks and the paw prints—but not the hair. Good job. Steve asked a neighboring municipality to make a cast of the tire tracks since we don't have the equipment."

"Oh."

"Let me put what you have in evidence. If it contains hair from either of the missing dogs, it could tie the car to the dognaper."

Relief washed through me. "Thank you."

I looked around for Steve, but I didn't see him in his office. That was okay. I was here to help. Since neither Steve nor Nash had any obligation to tell me the results, I thanked him again and left. I had to get cleaned up for my dad's birthday party.

About an hour before the festivities were to begin, I gathered my two presents, my prepared sides, and of course, Iggy.

"You do realize you can't sit at the table, right?" I told him.

"I know. I understand that there will be other people there who might freak out if they see a lizard on the table, but

I am willing to wash my feet beforehand."

I laughed. "I'll leave my purse open, so you can hear everything."

"Did you sign my name to the birthday card, at least?" Iggy asked.

"I did. You are part of our family."

"I'm glad to know you believe that."

I was pleased he didn't ask if Aimee would be there since Aunt Fern had been invited. I didn't think this party was the right place to introduce Aimee to the family, but that wasn't my decision.

Once I had everything packed, I went next door. I actually used the outside staircase to the second floor for a change instead of going through the closed funeral home and up the back staircase. I knocked, and my mother answered a minute later. Considering how long it took her to answer, she had probably been in the kitchen.

"Glinda. You're early."

She was always accusing me of never arriving on time. "I wanted to see if there was anything I could do to help?"

"No, sweetie. I have everything under control."

That was her usual refrain. We Goodall women rarely admitted we needed help. The funeral home was closed on Mondays, which gave Mom plenty of time to get things done. Despite throwing a party for quite a few people, she did appear to be calm. "Does that mean you might have a minute to do a quick contact?"

"Is that why you came early?"

"No." Yes. I wouldn't have asked, but Mom did enjoy that aspect of her life. It allowed her to be more creative than just doing bills and setting up the funeral schedule.

"All right, sweetie. Who do you need to contact?" she asked.

"Morgan Oliver. I know he said he never wanted to be contacted again, but I think he might have crossed over, so it's not like I can find him and talk to him." Jaxson and I had helped find who had murdered him, which meant he kind of owed us.

"I can try, but what do you hope to accomplish?"

"Maybe he knows something about these missing dogs."

My mother dipped her head and looked at me above her glasses. "Why would he know?"

"I don't know. Maybe he enjoys floating around. He might have learned something from the other ghosts." I didn't even believe ghosts existed until recently when I met the deceased Morgan Oliver. "I'm hoping he wants to give something back since I helped him."

She chuckled. "I'll give it a try, but we'll need to go downstairs where I have my candles and such."

I hugged my mother. "Thank you!"

Once she set up, she invited me to join her. "Since you and Morgan were close, at least in death, let's hold hands. It might make a stronger connection."

I couldn't remember the last time she'd invited me to join her. I could understand why she hadn't since I rarely knew the deceased. I wouldn't deny that this was exciting for me.

After she placed the herbs around the candles and then lit the wicks, we held hands. Unsure what I was supposed to do, I let my mother do the heavy lifting. When she closed her eyes, I followed suit. While this séance came with no instructions, I figured I should probably picture the first time I'd met Morgan.

My breath nearly stopped when his image appeared in my mind's eye. As much as I wanted to open my eyes to see if he really was in the room, I didn't want to chance breaking the connection.

"Hello, Glinda," he said.

I tightened my grip on my mother's hands. I expected her to say something, but she didn't. As strange as I felt talking to Morgan when I believed this ghost was in my mind, I went ahead anyway. Mom usually talked out loud, so I did also. "Do you know anything about the missing dogs?" I asked.

If he questioned which dogs, I'd know he had been blissfully enjoying the afterlife. His smile was brief. "Yes, but there are rules."

"Rules?" What was he talking about?

"If I give you all the answers you seek, where would the nobility be in your life? How much satisfaction would you gain if the solutions came easily?"

Seriously? I handed him his killer. Why couldn't he give me the names of the kidnappers? Protesting wouldn't do any good, however, mostly because what he said was true. It was how we overcame our struggles in life that provided us with our biggest joys—or so my grandmother used to preach. "Probably not much."

Keeping a looser grasp on my mother's hands, I leaned back.

"I'll tell you one thing. I owe you that much, and then we are even."

He was keeping score? "What is that?"

"Listen to the dog."

Before I could ask which dog, he was gone. My mother let go of my hands. "I can't sense him anymore," she said. "What did he say?"

"You couldn't hear him?"

"No, sweetie. This was a private conversation between you two."

"I thought you were the medium."

"I am. I brought him here, but he spoke only to you."

That was a difficult concept to understand, but it was what happened. "He said to listen to the dog."

"What does that mean? Which dog?" she asked.

I placed my palms on the table, pushed back my chair, and stood. "If I knew that, I could solve this case."

Chapter Twelve

A S SOON AS my mother and I cleaned up after the séance, we rushed upstairs to finish the preparations for the party. The guests would be arriving soon.

"Can you set out the glasses? Put out ones for water as well as for wine."

Wine, huh? This was going to be fancy. It wasn't often she served wine with dinner. Then again, my father, who had been looking pale for the last few days, might not have that many more birthdays to celebrate. To think he was only fifty really shook me up. But I was determined to paint on a happy face.

I counted the chairs. "There are two extra seats," I called to my mom, who was in the kitchen.

She came out, wiping her hands on her apron. "We invited Horace Crumfield, as well as a friend of your fathers."

"Horace? Really?"

"Yes. Your father depends on getting good discounts from him."

I didn't believe that was the only reason he was invited. Horace was about thirty-six—ten years older than me—and he had inherited the coffin-making business from his father who had inherited it from his dad. Don't get me wrong, the world needed coffins, especially my family who was in the funeral business, but Horace? He just wasn't my type.

I might be jumping the gun here though. I was assuming Mom, who was a hopeless matchmaker like everyone else in town, had invited him for me. She was always going on and on about when I would find a guy and settle down. Personally, I didn't think I needed a man to *complete me*—like Tom Cruise famously commented in *Jerry McGuire*.

While Horace wasn't bad looking, he had the personality of the dead. It might be the lighting, but I swear he wore light foundation to give the appearance of one who understood the needs of the dearly departed.

"Does my father's friend have a name? And do I know him?"

"I doubt it, sweetie. I've not met him either, but your father asked him."

Hold the presses. "Dad has friends?"

I know that sounded bad, but the only people he spoke with were grieving family members of the deceased. Other than going out once a month with the couple who ran the local flower shop, my parents were homebodies.

"Your father recently realized that he lacked any kind of life outside of the funeral home, and he wanted to do something about it."

"Good for him."

My mother didn't have much a life outside of the house either, unless I counted her monthly coven meetings—ones she wanted me to attend—as social outings. Being a lousy witch, I didn't want to be surrounded by highly competent women. I had my own abilities, ones that didn't revolve solely around contacting the dead or doing spells.

"What does this new life of his entail?" I asked.

"Hunting."

I almost choked. "Hunting? As in he uses a gun to shoot a rabbit?" I'm sure he'd never shoot a deer. "I thought he hated the idea of harming animals."

"His hunts are not inhumane. He says he uses a bow and arrow. Or maybe it's a crossbow. I really don't remember what he told me."

My mom wasn't the best listener, but I doubt she got the hunting part wrong. I still couldn't imagine my father being in the woods, let alone him using any kind of weapon. "What brought this on?"

"Like I told you. Your dad thinks he needs to get out more. He met Hunter Ashwell a while ago, and they immediately bonded. Since Hunter is some kind of forest ranger, your dad agreed to hunt with him."

That seemed so bogus, but who was I to say who should be friends with whom? "Good for him." I needed to brush up on my hunting knowledge, but I didn't think one could hunt in the summer. In need of a change in subject, I nodded to the table. "I like the centerpiece, by the way."

My mom smiled. "I know I've used it often, but your dad loves it so much."

I liked how this time mom had leaned Dorothy's red, sparkly shoes against the basket. The small stuffed animal that represented Toto was a bit overkill in my humble opinion, but it was still nice.

I doubted she did this because my dad loved it. Being devoted to all things having to do with *The Wizard of Oz*, my

mom had purchased many icons over the years that represented each of the main characters. Beside the shoes, the basket,
and Toto, she had the scarecrow's floppy hat, a silver painted
funnel to represent the tin man, a miniature pink hat like the
one Glinda wore in the movie, and a small stuffed lion. I had
to hand it to her: It was cute.

"What else can I do?" I asked. Just then the doorbell rang,
and I held up a finger. "I know, I'll answer the door." I hoped
it was someone I wanted to talk to. I pulled it open and
smiled. It was Tim and Sheila Oglethorpe, the ones who
owned the flower shop that was situated in the same strip of
stores next to the movie theater "Hey there. Come in."

Sheila had a small wrapped present. "Where should I put
this?"

"I put mine on the sideboard behind the table."

Mom stepped up to them. "Tim and Sheila." She hugged
each of them. My mother turned to me. "Can you let your
dad know people are arriving?"

"Sure." Most likely he was in his study, where he liked to
sit and read. As I've mentioned, he was a low-key type of guy,
not one to run around a forest hunting!

I found him on the phone in his office. "Sure, I understand. No problem. Thanks for calling."

"Who was that?" I asked.

"Horace. He had to cancel. He has a last-minute coffin to
build."

That excuse didn't sound all that plausible, but who was I
to say? "Happy birthday, Dad."

He looked up and smiled. "Thank you, sweetie."

"The Oglethorpes are here. Mom said it's time to get the

party going. I believe dinner is almost ready."

He slowly leveraged himself out of the chair. I stepped over to him. "Are you okay?"

When he smiled, he looked like his old self. "Never better."

Since this was his birthday, I didn't want to harp on him about slowing down or getting checked out by a doctor. Fifty was still very young, but my dad hadn't aged well. "Then let's go."

Dad immediately started chatting with the Oglethorpes. Mom motioned to me. "Glinda, help me carry out the food."

I was happy to oblige. I'd just taken my casserole from the oven when Aunt Fern came in. "There you two are," she said. "Wendy, what can I do to help?" she asked my mom.

"Put your items on the table, unless they need to be heated."

"Nope. Everything's warm."

My mom removed the rolls from the oven and placed them in the special basket. Within minutes, we had the food on the table. Just as we were about to sit down, the doorbell rang again. I didn't need my mother to ask me to answer it. It was my usual job.

This had to be Hunter Ashwell. Because my dad was fifty, I kind of expected this guy to be too. Instead, he looked to be in his thirties. He was close to six feet and rather buff. It was probably the chiseled jaw that gave him the rugged look of a man who was at home in the forest.

At first glance, his eyes looked red, but when he turned his head, they were dark brown. My imagination must have been going wild. "You must be Hunter," I said. "I'm Glinda.

Come in."

He stepped inside. When he glanced at the pile of presents, he hesitated. "I didn't know we were supposed to bring a gift."

"You weren't. You have to have known my dad for at least five years before it is expected." I smiled, and as I'd hoped, he chuckled. I could see why he was a forest ranger. I always imagined his kind to be rather chill—and that fit Hunter to a tee. "Come in. We're just about to eat."

"Sorry I was late."

I couldn't help but laugh. "That's usually my line."

"I'll think of you as my partner in crime then." He winked.

I didn't want to like him, but I did. We entered the dining room together. My mother had removed the seat meant for Horace, and what do you know, the two remaining seats where next to each other. A friend of my father's indeed. This was probably who my mom really wanted to fix me up with, despite her not knowing him. I considered showing him Iggy to let him know who I was, but I wouldn't do that to my dad. If these two truly were friends, I needed to support that.

My mom made the usual introductions, and a fair amount of questions were thrown out and answered by all at the table.

About half way through the meal, I finally couldn't control my curiosity about the one topic that hadn't been discussed. "Dad, Mom tells me you've taken up hunting."

"I haven't done any real hunting yet. Hunter is showing me how to use a crossbow. Hunting season doesn't begin for a few months."

At least he was being responsible about following the law. "Is it a class?"

"It is," Hunter said, answering instead. "I'm a forest ranger. Safety is one of my major concerns. Too often people are injured because they fail to use the equipment correctly."

That sounded feasible. "How did you and my dad meet?"

They exchanged looks. My father answered. "At church."

I rarely went, so that would be something I wouldn't be able to corroborate—unless I dug, which I wouldn't. "I see."

"Glinda," my mom said. "Why don't you tell everyone about the missing dog case?"

If that wasn't a misdirect, I didn't know what was. I obliged, but I made sure to leave out a lot of the details. Hunter or the Oglethorpes didn't need to hear about my visit to Gertrude or to Jack Hanson. I don't know why I didn't feel the need to tell them, but the vibe in the room seemed a bit off.

"I was talking with Sarah the other day," Sheila said. "Her dog was supposed to compete. She mentioned in passing that she hoped Amy didn't win." The florist's lips pursed.

I'd interacted with Sarah many times. She owned the yarn shop, and because she was always so pleasant, I couldn't imagine her making that kind of negative statement. "Why would she say that?"

Sheila leaned forward. "Apparently, Amy taught Sarah's daughter this past year, and Amy wasn't very nice to her."

"Oh." It wasn't often that I was speechless. "Did Sarah say anything else?"

"She mentioned that Warren Wilson was an odd duck. His dog is a Whippet named Tinkerbell. I mean, who calls a dog Tinkerbell?"

Who calls their dog Snookums? My opinion of Sheila dropped a few notches, but I wasn't about to ask her to stop gossiping. She might really know something. "Maybe the dog already had that name when he bought him." I always tried to find the good in people.

Sheila shook her head. "Sarah thinks he stole the dog."

I sucked in a breath. "Why would she think that?"

Sheila lifted one shoulder. "I didn't ask."

I didn't believe that for a New York minute. How had I not seen this side of Sheila before? My mother was glaring at me instead of at her gossipy friend.

"Glinda, help me clear the table, please."

I knew that tone. "Happy to."

My aunt pushed back her chair too and picked up two plates. Between the three of us, the table was cleared in record time.

Once in the kitchen, my mom turned to me. "What is wrong with you?"

"Me? What did I say? Sheila is the one who is spreading nasty rumors," I shot back. "Nothing is worse than being falsely accused of something."

"If she wants to spread a few rumors, let her, but questioning her in front of everyone is not nice. It's your father's birthday."

I would tone it down, but only because I didn't want to upset my dad. I couldn't help but go over what Sheila said about Amy and Warren though. I hoped for Nash's sake that he wasn't seriously dating Amy. She did seem to attract some negative attention.

While my aunt and I returned to the table, my mother gathered the presents and placed them in front of my father. I hoped to see a light turn on in my dad's eyes again.

My mother gave him a new wallet since he always seemed to wear his out. Aunt Fern bought him a gift card to the movies. I would have to thank her for that. Anything to get my dad out of the house was a good thing. He seemed to like the tie and cuff links I gave him, but truthfully, they looked like all the other blue or gray ties that he owned. The Oglethorpes presented him with a gift card to Miriam's coffee shop. All in all, my dad cleaned up for his birthday. By the time he'd finished with the gift giving, I saw that spark in his eyes again.

"I have an announcement," my aunt said when Mom had collected the presents and placed them on the sideboard.

We all turned to face her. Even Iggy popped his head out of my purse. Hunter caught sight of him, but he didn't comment. For that, he just earned a bonus point in my mind.

"What is it?" my mother asked.

"I agreed to go out on a date."

When I shifted my gaze to behind my aunt, Uncle Harold was standing behind her, smiling and nodding. If that wasn't an endorsement, I don't know what it was.

"That's fantastic. Who is the lucky man, Aunt Fern?" I was almost afraid to ask.

"Bob Hatfield."

I had to think who that was. The name sounded familiar. "Isn't he the one who was taking bets as to who would win the dog agility competition?"

"Yes, but most of the money goes to the animal shelter."

I wasn't sure what to say. "That's a worthy cause. How did you meet?" I don't recall her telling me she went to the show.

"Bob came into the restaurant two nights in a row."

What I wouldn't give to have been a fly on that wall. My aunt had been asked out on several occasions, but she'd turned everyone down without a backward glance. I never saw Bob at the park that first day, so I had no idea what he looked like. "What does he do for a living?"

"He's a hospital administrator."

Really? That sounded good. I'd have to ask Jaxson to check up on him—or maybe I'd ask Steve if the man had a criminal record. For his grandmother's good friend, he might be willing to do a little background check. "What about Harold?" I said, kind of under my breath.

Just because I had seen the ghost of my uncle smile, it didn't mean he was okay with this.

"Harold and I had a long talk. He's fine if I date again."

I glanced over at Hunter. I bet he was wondering what was going on, but it wasn't my place to fill him in. "I think it's great. When will this big event take place?"

"He's taking me to dinner Saturday night."

I hoped it wasn't to the Tiki Hut Grill. That would be beyond tacky. "Where are you two going?"

"I believe to the same steak house you and Jaxson went to in Holland." She winked.

I had to assume she was trying to let Hunter know I wasn't the free bird my mother probably led him to believe. Not that I was dating Jaxson, or anyone else for that matter, but this gave me a good out. For that I was thankful.

"I hope it works out."

She giggled. "So do I."

I pushed aside my reservations and smiled.

"Cake anyone?" my mom asked as she lit the birthday candles.

The group gave a resounding yes.

Chapter Thirteen

WORK THE NEXT day was a drag mostly because Tuesday was Penny's day off, and I missed our quick chats in between serving our sections. The only other thing that might have cheered me up was if Steve or Nash had come in for a bite to eat. Only they didn't. Not that I really expected them to, but it would have made the day more interesting.

After making certain no one at my tables needed me, I sidled over to my aunt, who was adding some gift items to the display case. I swear the woman could sell a bathing suit to someone from the North Pole.

"Has Bob stopped in today?" I asked.

"No, he's working."

"I forgot it's a weekday. Didn't you say he worked at the hospital?" I hadn't asked Jaxson or Steve to check up on this man. I think it was because I trusted my aunt.

"Yes."

"I'm curious to know what made you change your mind about dating?"

"Harold is tired. I think he wants to cross over."

I still didn't really understand how all that worked. "He told you that?"

"Not in so many words. He used to come down to the restaurant to chat every day. Then it became every other day. Eventually, his image would fade in and out. I truly believe he wanted to be here in order to provide me with comfort after he passed. Not that I don't still miss him; he said he can sense that I'm going to be okay. He told me it's been two years and that I need to get on with my life." She chuckled. "I don't know where he picked up that expression."

"I bet from Penny."

My aunt smiled. "I think you might be right. How is she doing by the way? You said she is maybe back with Sam?"

"Last Saturday was their first official date. I worry about her. She deserves a man who is more stable."

"You know what I always say," my aunt said.

"A leopard doesn't change its spots. I know, but people can change."

"You are right," she said.

I couldn't help but think of Jaxson. He had been so unsettled when he'd first arrived in Witch's Cove. Then circumstances changed, and he became someone who was quite light-hearted and fun to be with. What I worried about was that since Jaxson grew up troubled, I couldn't be sure he wouldn't return to his old ways. Dwelling on that, however, wouldn't be productive.

"What are your thoughts on Dad's friend, Hunter?" I asked.

"He is handsome," Aunt Fern winked.

"I agree that he's easy on the eyes, but good looks don't make a relationship. I know he's a forest ranger, so it makes sense he'd be teaching a course of hunting safety, but I didn't realize they were such good friends."

She quickly sobered. "I agree. Something is fishy. I wish I knew what's bothering me about it."

I waved a hand. "Let's forget it. If Dad wants to hunt, I should be happy that he is getting out of the funeral home."

"Your father gets away, trust me."

My heart dropped to my stomach. "What does that mean? I realize of late I haven't stopped by as often as I used to, but Mom would have said if Dad was merely out and about."

Aunt Fern shrugged. "He leaves every four weeks for a day or two."

She was keeping track? My brain jumped to a very bad conclusion. I leaned close. "Are you saying you think Dad is having an affair?"

My aunt huffed. "Oh, heavens no. He only has eyes for your mother."

"Then what?" My parents were one of the stable things in my life—them and my aunt. I couldn't handle it if their relationship fell apart.

"I'm not sure. I'm going to assume that your dad goes to the forest to take those hunting lessons during those times, though the timing doesn't quite line up." She waved a hand. "I say we shouldn't worry about it.

I rolled my eyes. "Fine, but I still don't picture Dad ever killing a deer."

"I agree that seems unlikely, but it's hard for a man your dad's age to find a sport that doesn't require a lot of physical stamina."

"That's true. I don't see him taking up jogging or joining an indoor basketball league, but what about golf?"

"I actually suggested that, but he said it was too expensive."

If he was looking into hobbies, maybe this was the best solution. "Did mom suggest he get out of the house? I know dealing with grief all day can haunt the soul."

"She did. Even now she's worried about him. And so am I."

Just then two of my tables filled up. "Gotta go. Any snooping about Dad is appreciated."

Aunt Fern laughed and went back to arranging the display case.

The rest of the afternoon was business as usual. I was confident that Steve and Nash were working the missing dog case, but I had one more thing to check out. Tomorrow was Maude and Miriam's big celebration. If Steve came, it might give me a chance to casually mention that Aunt Fern was dating the man who was taking the bets on the dog show. I know I said I trusted my aunt, but what if he was only after her for her money? It didn't feel as if he should be considered a suspect in the dog case since it would be in his best interest to have all seven dogs compete, but I'd be remiss if I didn't at least ask Steve about him. As a hospital administrator, he should have plenty of money. However, for all I knew, he could have three ex-wives and lots of alimony to pay.

Once I clocked out, I went upstairs to change. Iggy was on the kitchen counter eating some wilted lettuce that I apparently had forgotten to put away last night.

He looked up. "We never got to chat about Aunt Fern's new beau. What do you think of him?"

I was surprised he didn't rib me about Hunter. "I know

nothing about him."

"You need to ask Dolly."

I stilled. "Why would she know?" True, Dolly and my aunt had vied for the same man in the past.

He did that leg lift thing that I believed was akin to a shrug. "She knows a lot."

Iggy could be right. It might be worthwhile stopping in. "Aunt Fern said he worked at the hospital as an administrator. Is that consistent with what you know?"

"Your aunt has not breathed a word to me about him."

Interesting. "Then I'll check with Dolly."

"Smart, but I want to go with you. I'm bored," Iggy said.

"Really?"

"I promise I won't complain. Besides, Dolly's diner has really good lettuce."

"Fine." I grabbed my larger purse. Once he was settled inside, I grabbed my wallet, keys, and phone then headed out.

"I need to make one stop before going to the diner."

Iggy poked his head out and looked around. "Where?"

"To Silas Adams' music shop. It faces the park. If anyone has a good view of the comings and goings in recent days, it would be him."

"Cool."

I didn't have high hopes of gathering pertinent information, but I had to try.

A chime sounded as I stepped into his store. Silas was around seventy, but his grizzled beard and arthritic hands made him appear older. Many years ago, I had taken music lessons from his wife, Kathy. She was so sweet—the opposite of Mr. Adams. Back then, I was afraid of him. Considering how he looked, I still might be.

"Afternoon," he said, his tone anything but cordial.

Since I was the only customer, I would have thought he'd have been a bit more friendly. It appeared as if he didn't recognize me. "Hi, I'm Glinda Goodall. I used to take piano classes from your wife." I smiled.

"Is that so?" He didn't sound impressed.

"Is everything okay?" I asked. The man seemed depressed.

"All the noise and fuss from the dog show drove away my customers."

Considering the dog show was canceled and he had no customers now, I didn't see how the show made a difference. "Is that so?"

"You bet. A lot of people came in asking to use the bathroom, but then no one bought anything."

I had been worried about that. Even though he was rather disgruntled, I was hoping he was the type to look out his window. "By any chance did you see that car that drove over the sidewalk onto the soggy park grass?" I stepped to the window and pointed to the area where I'd seen the tire tracks.

"I sure did. The man should be issued a ticket."

My pulse jacked up. "I totally agree. People don't respect boundaries. What kind of car was it?"

"It was a white van, one of those long ones without windows."

That might have been a commercial vehicle. "How long was it parked for?"

"Ten minutes. I watched the whole thing. Nothing upsets me more than people breaking the rules. In fact, I was about to call the sheriff and complain when I saw Lassie walk right up to the mangy dude and get in the back. I figured if he had a dog, he couldn't be all bad."

"Lassie? You knew this dog?" Darn, and here I thought he might have provided the break in the case.

He waved a hand. "I don't know the dog's name, but it was the same kind of breed as Lassie."

There used to be an old TV show by that name. "Do you mean a collie?"

"Yeah."

This was too good to be true. "What did the man look like?"

"I didn't pay much attention. He looked homeless to me. He probably lived out of his van."

A customer came in, and Mr. Silas faced him. "Be right with you," he said.

I knew when it was time to go. "Thanks."

With this information, I had to tell Steve and Nash. Sure, Steve had ordered casts to be made of the tire tracks, but it might help if I could tell them it was a white van, and that this vehicle had most likely been responsible for taking Mittens.

Chapter Fourteen

I STRODE DOWN the street to the sheriff's office. Once more, only Nash was in the office.

"Back so soon?" he said as he stood and walked toward the front.

I explained about my discussion with Silas Adams. "He said that he saw a collie get in a white van that was parked where I, or rather we, spotted the muddy tire tracks."

His brows rose, but the rest of his face remained expressionless. "Did he get a look at the driver?"

"That was the iffy part. He just said the guy looked homeless."

"I appreciate the heads up. I may have a chat with Mr. Silas. Good work."

Pleasure shot through me. Nothing gave me a bigger high than finding a clue. "Thanks."

With Iggy in tow, we headed to the Spellbound Diner. Even if the owner had no gossip for me, I was looking forward to a shake.

When I walked in, only about half of the booths were taken, and Dolly was behind the counter. When she saw me, she smiled and waved. I was happy that the competition between my aunt and her did not extend to me.

I took a seat and checked the menu, deciding to go with an old-fashioned chocolate shake. Dolly came over and, as was her usual style, she slid in across from me. She did that with many of her customers. I think that personal touch was what made people return time and time again.

"What's up?" she asked.

I decided not to beat around the bush about my aunt. I didn't feel the need to mention the white van and the scruffy man just yet, since it was now in the hands of Witch's Cove finest. "Aunt Fern dropped a bomb on us last night."

Her eyes widened. "Tell me."

I laughed at her enthusiasm. "She has a date Saturday night."

"Shut the front door."

That was code for are you kidding me? I crossed my heart and held up my palm to swear it was the truth. "That's what she said."

"Who's the guy?"

"Bob Hatfield. Do you know him?"

"Sure do."

Oh, goodie. I waited for some kind of explanation, but none came. "Is he an okay guy? Or should I be worried for Aunt Fern?"

"His latest wife died about three years ago. He works at the hospital. Seems nice, not that I've had any long conversations with him."

Before she could tell me anything else, the dog trainer of the recently canceled competition came through the door and checked out who was there. "Don't turn around," I said, "but Diana Upton just came in."

"The dog trainer?"

"The one and only." I'd checked her out, as well as the other dog owners, after Steve gave me the list of names. Diana was still wearing her pink and white bandana around her neck, which, if I had to guess, was her signature piece. "Steve said he had asked all of the people involved with the show to stick around for a few days if they didn't live in or near Witch's Cove."

"Good to know. Let me see what she wants." Dolly smiled. "But first, what do you want?"

"A chocolate shake. Oh yeah, and some lettuce for Iggy." I nodded to my purse.

"You got it."

Diana slid into a booth near the entrance. While it was at the other end of the diner from where I was seated, I could easily keep an eye on her. I wondered if she was meeting anyone or if she was there to eat alone? I don't know what it was about finding something new that got my blood pumping. I think I might have been born a sleuth.

"What is she doing?" Iggy asked.

The booth right in front of hers was empty. "I'd love to know. Do you want to do some spying?"

That was a dumb question, but I had to ask.

"Do you like pink?"

I chuckled. "Okay, when Dolly returns, I'll have her carry my purse over to the booth in front of Diana's. Do not show yourself. Just listen."

"Yes, ma'am."

Iggy knew I didn't like that moniker, but I'd let it go this time. In the meantime, I studied Diana. She pulled out a tissue from her purse and swiped it under her eyes. Don't ask me why, but I didn't think she was crying over the missing dogs. No one had even mentioned that she'd searched for them. With all of her contacts, I would have thought she'd have some idea who might have taken them, especially if any dogs had gone missing in other shows.

Now more than ever, I wish I could find out what Nash had learned about the list I gave him, but since this was an ongoing investigation, he wouldn't tell me.

Dolly slid in across from Diana and pulled out her pad. I couldn't hear what they said, but I was sure Dolly would repeat it word for word when she returned.

I was glad the news about Bob Hatfield had been neutral. I would hate to have to tell my aunt she might be making a mistake.

Dolly was taking quite a long time chatting with the trainer. Hurry up! When the owner returned to the counter, Dolly made my order. With my drink in hand, along with a piece of lettuce, she came over and set it in front of me.

"So?" I whispered.

"She doesn't know anything about the missing dogs. She's sad and anxious about them. I don't blame her for thinking this might cause other vendors to stop supporting these shows."

I guess I had been wrong about her. "That's a good point. If the shows go away, so does her job."

Dolly nodded. "To make matters worse, Diana has another competition to go to across the state. Naturally, she wants Steve to solve the case, so she can return to work."

"That makes sense. Thanks for asking." I lifted my purse.

"Can you do me a favor?"

I explained about wanting Iggy to have a chance to spy on Diana should she call someone.

"No problem, but it might not be a phone call. She said she was waiting for someone," Dolly said.

"That's even better."

After giving him his leaf, Dolly took my purse, and to her credit, she was quite stealthy about placing it on the seat in front of Diana's booth. Iggy had to be really excited.

I took my time sipping my drink, enjoying the rich flavor, waiting for the mystery guest to arrive. Less than five minutes later, a man with disheveled brown hair, wearing rather dirty jeans slid across from her. Unfortunately, his back was to me, so I couldn't study his face. I was really tempted to text Steve to let him know there was a slim chance the van owner was at the diner, but without proof on my part, he'd dismiss me.

I couldn't hear the conversation, but Diana Upton did not seem happy. She was pointing a finger at the man with her brows pinched. He leaned forward and said something. I really hoped Iggy was hearing all of this. Diana opened her purse, threw down some money, even though she hadn't ordered anything, and left.

Okay. I hadn't expected that. The man slid out of the booth and rushed after her. Something had just gone down, and it took a few minutes for my heart to slow. Since Diana had left and didn't appear to be returning, I retrieved Iggy. I couldn't wait to hear what he had to say. Talking to my purse might rouse some suspicions, so I quickly finished off my drink, paid, and rushed down the street to find Drake and Jaxson. I wanted them to hear Iggy's news.

Tuesday was usually a slow day for the shop, and today wasn't an exception. Good for me but not for him.

Drake greeted me with a smile. "Hey, how did your dad's birthday party go?" he asked.

"It was complicated. And you?" Instead of rushing into my news, I waited for him to tell me how his day had gone.

"I have just the thing to cheer you up. This morning, I received a shipment of some blue cheese I've been dying to try. Care to join me?"

I loved blue cheese, and Drake knew it. I didn't have the heart to tell him I'd just eaten something. "Sure."

He sliced a few pieces and placed them on a plate along with some crackers. "Dig in."

The smell was heavenly, and it tasted even better. "I needed this."

"Tell me what's on your mind," Drake said, despite me asking about his day.

I didn't ask if Jaxson was there, because in all honesty, I enjoyed being with my best friend again. It was the way it used to be.

Iggy popped his head up. "What are you doing? I need to tell you two something. And it's really important."

"Okay, okay." I explained as quickly as possible about visiting Silas Adams and his description of the van. "After I told Nash about it, I stopped in at the diner. Diana Upton showed up."

"Who?" Drake asked.

I admit it was hard to keep all of the names straight. "The dog trainer."

"Oh, yes. Go on."

"After waiting a few minutes, a man joined her."

"Did you recognize him?" Drake asked.

"No, but he could have been the van owner. Don't worry, Iggy heard the entire conversation."

"Finally," my cute pink iguana said.

I waited until Iggy relayed the conversation to me before I told Drake what he said. "Thank you, Iggy. You were amazing." Though their discussion was a bit cryptic.

"What did he say?" Drake asked.

"Diana wanted a bigger cut of the profits. Without her, this man would have no animals."

His mouth dropped open. "Does that mean she was involved in stealing the dogs?"

"That would be my guess."

"You have to tell the sheriff."

I inhaled. "I would, but Steve would ask what proof I have."

"I can testify," Iggy said.

"That would be great, except that no one can hear you."

He slipped back down into my purse. Poor thing.

"Now what?" Drake asked.

"In theory, she isn't leaving town. If Steve or Nash find the van's owner, I might say something."

"Good."

Not ready to leave, I told him about my father taking up hunting. No surprise, Drake was stunned.

"That doesn't sound like him."

"I know, but if it gets him out of the house, I'm happy."

"You say that, but your eyes aren't confirming it."

He was too perceptive. "You're right. What I wouldn't

give to find someone who was in this class so I could pick their brain. I'd even be willing to learn how to use a crossbow if it meant I could keep an eye on my dad."

Drake looked at me. "What's really going on?"

"You'll think I'm crazy."

He laughed. "Glinda, nothing you do or say would make me think that."

He was the sweetest man. "Okay. According to Aunt Fern, Dad leaves every month for a couple of days. I didn't ask what time of the month it was or if these dates were on the same day."

"But?" he asked.

"Do you remember what Emma Paxton told us about her husband?"

"Glinda Goodall, don't tell me you think your father is a werewolf!"

I instantly reacted. "No. Maybe. What other explanation is there? He's been looking very pale lately."

"I'm not up on my werewolf lore, but once a werewolf feeds, the blood boosts his energy."

I grabbed his arm. "You're right. My dad would have to be pale one week and look robust the next."

"If that's the case, maybe he's a vampire." Drake winked and then turned more serious. "Or...maybe he leaves because the classes he's taking meet on the same day of the month. Ever think of that?"

I leaned against the counter. "I hope you're right, but I think this has been going on for longer than the classes."

"You should ask him," Drake said.

"I'm not ready to do that yet. It's the change in his health

128

that really bothers me."

"He could be anemic. A doctor could tell. Come on. Let's finish the cheese and crackers. It will help clear your brain."

That was what I loved about my friend. He could erase my worry. We delved into the culinary delight, and I had to admit the burst of flavor raised my spirits. "I plan to mark the calendar when he leaves and compare it to the full moon."

Drake shook his head and smiled. "I do love your imagination. You make life so much more exciting."

He was probably mocking me, but that was okay. I did feel better after expressing my concern. "On a different note," I said. "Aunt Fern has a date with this guy, Bob Hatfield."

"That is newsworthy. I didn't think your aunt would ever go out again."

"Me neither, but she said she doesn't want Harold to have to stay around for longer than necessary."

"You don't seem all that excited about this new development," Drake said as he stuffed another cracker in his mouth and then washed it down with some water.

"I don't know enough about him, but I worry about her."

"Why? Your aunt is a smart lady."

"I know."

"If it will make you feel better, I'll ask Jaxson to look into him," Drake said.

My relief took me by surprise. "I'd appreciate that." We always seemed to talk about my problems, and that wasn't fair to Drake. "Tell me what you've been up to."

"Same old, same old."

"You do realize all work and no play makes Drake a dull boy?"

He planted a hand on his chest. "Me? Dull? Is that what you are implying?"

I did adore him. "No. I just thought between Trace and Jaxson working here that you could have some time to yourself. Surely, there must be someone you're interested in?"

"Don't you start and play matchmaker."

I held up a hand and smiled. "I get it." I grinned. "Hey, maybe you could take up crossbow lessons."

He wagged a finger at me. "I can see right through you, Glinda Goodall. You want someone to spy on your dad."

I huffed out a breath. "Is that so bad?"

"Yes, it is. Now, let's get back to your obsession. Are you sure you aren't going to mention the argument Diana had with this stranger to the good sheriff?"

"Not right now. I just wished I had taken the guy's picture. I would have only captured the back of his head, but that could have helped."

Drake laughed. "You are something else."

"You know what I'm going to do?" I asked. He shook his head. "I plan to focus on enjoying myself at Maude and Miriam's tea and coffee party tomorrow."

He smiled. "Good for you."

"I will stay out of the investigation unless some major clue drops into my lap."

"Sure, Glinda. Sure."

Drake knew me too well.

Chapter Fifteen

A FTER FILLING UP on cheese and crackers, I was ready to head to bed and indulge in a good book. I'd just stepped into my bedroom when there was a knock on my front door, startling me. The force of the rap indicated it was a man. If Jaxson had discovered something, he would have called.

I approached with caution. "Who is it?" I asked as I looked through the peephole. Oh, my goodness. My pulse skyrocketed for a second, and then I relaxed.

"It's Steve and Nash."

I was thankful he didn't say it was the Witch's Cove sheriff's department. Then I would have thought they were there to arrest me—for something I didn't do, mind you. Or had he heard about my snooping with Diana Upton?

I hadn't changed into my pajamas yet, so I pulled open the door. Seeing both men in uniform made my heart drop to my stomach. This visit seemed too official. In my mind, the cops came to a person's door to report a death of a loved one. "Did something happen?"

"Yes," Steve said. "May we come in?"

"Of course."

I glanced over at Iggy, hoping he wouldn't cause a stir. "Can I get you something to drink?" I asked with a very dry mouth.

"This isn't a social visit, Glinda."

I figured as much. I didn't ask if they wanted to sit, because they would probably say no. I, however, had to because my legs were about to give way. "What is this about?"

Steve looked at Nash. "I have to say, I'm surprised you haven't heard."

Clearly, my reputation continued to follow me. "Heard what?"

"Diana Upton, the trainer, is missing."

"Missing?" Only a small part of me relaxed since he didn't tell me something horrible like Penny or one of the Harrison brothers had been seriously injured or killed. "I just saw her at Dolly's diner."

"When was this?" Nash asked as he pulled out his notepad.

"Maybe two hours ago. Why do you think she's missing?"

"Brad Thomas, the one who had signed up to compete with his Golden Retriever, Randy, needed to get a hold of her. They were supposed to meet an hour ago, but she didn't show up."

I didn't think that sounded too serious, nor did I think her not showing up to a rendezvous warranted a visit by the sheriff's department. Didn't a person have to be missing for twenty-four hours before they started looking? I suppose with the dogs disappearing, they thought foul play might be involved. "Maybe she decided not to talk to him."

"Maybe. We looked in her hotel room. Her clothes, purse, and car keys are still there."

Okay, now that sounded bad. "Are you thinking someone

kidnapped her, like they did the dogs?"

"That was our thought, but we have no proof." I had never seen Steve so serious.

"If that's true, it gives me hope the dogs might still be alive. They might need her to take care of them."

"We tried her cell, but she isn't answering."

"I often let my cell phone go to voicemail," I said. I then told him about the man she met at the diner. "She looked angry. I couldn't hear everything other than her demanding more money for the operation." I looked over at Iggy.

"That's about right," he said.

"What operation?" Steve asked as Nash jotted down some notes.

"I don't know. She didn't stay long enough to order anything. She tossed down some money, and the man followed her out."

"What did the man look like?" Nash asked.

I knew they had to ask these questions, but it almost felt as if I was being interrogated. "I only saw the back of his head."

"Was he bald, have long hair, or what?" Nash asked.

"He was unkempt. His curly brown hair looked as if he hadn't combed it in a while. I did notice his jeans were dirty."

Nash continued to take notes. "That kind of sounds like the man Silas Adams described," Steve said.

"I know, right? I thought the same thing."

Steve leveled me with a stare. "Why didn't you report it?"

I knew the answer to that one. "You would have said I had no proof that the man in the diner was the same one who took the dog and drove off in a white van."

He nodded. "I'm sorry. You're right. Anything else you can tell us?"

I replayed everything in my mind. "No, I'm sorry."

Steve nodded. "I'm worried about Diane's safety. If you hear anything, and I mean anything, please let us know."

I stood. "I promise."

Once they left, I shut and locked the door. I felt a little guilty that I hadn't said anything sooner, but no one knew whether this man had anything to do with her disappearance—assuming she really was missing and not in hiding—or even with the dogs' disappearance.

"What are you going to do?" Iggy asked.

"Me? What can I do?"

"You could talk to Gertrude."

"You think she might have had another vision?" I asked.

"It's possible. She knew about the two dogs."

I checked my watch and realized it was quite late. Considering her advanced age, she was probably in bed. "I'll contact her tomorrow morning, though if she had another pink aura vision, she would have called." Or so I'd hoped.

My cell rang a few minutes later, and every nerve shot to life. My phone was in the bedroom. "Excuse me."

My ever-curious lizard followed me into the room. For once, I didn't mind having the company. I checked the caller ID. It was Penny. Since I didn't have to work tomorrow, she probably figured I would be up.

"Hey. Is everything okay?" I asked. I seemed to have a sixth sense when it came to Penny. Super bad news meant she'd come to the apartment. Semi bad news often came in the form of late-night phone calls.

"No, it's not. It's Sam."

I needed to sit on the bed for this conversation. Sad to say, I had anticipated their new relationship would be filled with pitfalls. "What happened?"

"He came over to my place after he'd been drinking. He was rude. I really thought he'd changed, but he hasn't. I am such a fool."

I was happy to take my mind off of Diana Upton for a moment. It would give me a chance to figure out my next move. Right now, Penny needed me. "You weren't a fool. You were hopeful. I am so sorry, Penny. I know how much you wanted this to work. What are you going to do?" I asked.

"What can I do? I have Tommy to think of. I told him I didn't think it would work out between me and his dad. Needless to say, our son was not happy."

My chest squeezed. "Sam wasn't violent with you, was he?"

"No, no. He yelled loud enough to wake up Tommy though, but then he was very contrite when our son came out of his room. But, Glinda, I can't go through this again."

"Of course not." This was one more reason not to date—at least for now.

"I don't mean to be such a downer, but it's really hard raising a child by myself."

I'd heard that refrain a lot, and I understood how hard it might be. "At least your mom helps out."

"She does."

I wasn't sure what she thought I could do. "If I had any talent doing love potions, I would mix up a batch and let you give it to whoever you fancied."

She nearly squealed. "You are a genius."

Uh-oh. I was only kidding. The problem was that Penny was often impulsive. "What are you going to do? And please don't say you want to put a spell on Sam."

"No, silly, but if I find a guy I like, I wouldn't object to giving him something to make him notice me."

I didn't like where this was headed. "Penny."

"Don't worry. I wouldn't do that." She sighed. "Or maybe I would. Oh, Glinda. I want a real relationship."

"Your time will come." How many times had we said that to each other? Answer? Too many to count.

"Thanks for cheering me up."

I don't think I said anything significant, but if she was happy, so was I. "You're welcome."

"Do you have plans on your day off tomorrow?" she asked.

"I'm not sure." A least none that I was willing to share just yet. I needed to confer with Gertrude about what might have happened to Diana.

"Have you given up looking for the missing dogs then?"

Why did everyone think I was obsessed with solving cases? "Steve and Nash are working on it."

"I get it. If you get bored, you can always stop downstairs and chat."

"I'll do that. I trust you are going to go to Maude and Miriam's annual opening celebration tomorrow night?"

"Are you kidding? I wouldn't miss it. Last year, everyone was saying that Miriam outdid Maude. I heard Maude plans to outdo her sister this year."

I laughed. "As competitive as they are with each other,

underneath it all, they do seem to adore each other."

"I know. The sad part is that all they have is each other," Penny said.

"I disagree. Given all the friends they have, their lives are rich."

"You're probably right. Thanks again. I'm going to hit the sack. Gotta get up early tomorrow."

"Sleep well." I sighed as I disconnected.

"What did she say?" Iggy asked as soon as I placed the phone on the nightstand.

"Nothing much, except that she and Sam are no longer an item."

"I bet that hurt," he said, his voice sounding more distant than usual.

At first, I wanted to ask what he knew about emotional pain, but then I realized he was pining for Aimee. "I'm sorry Aimee isn't returning your affection."

"That's okay. She'll come around. As you said, she is a cat."

Cats could be highly affectionate. They also could be very independent and happy to be alone, which often made them look cold or snooty.

THE NEXT MORNING, I went over to the Psychics Corner, hoping Gertrude was free. I didn't think she'd had another vision, because she didn't try to contact me, but I would be remiss if I didn't check it out.

Because it was early, the lobby was empty. Thankfully,

Sarah was there.

"Glinda! Who is it going to be today?"

I was becoming a pest. "I really need to speak with Gertrude. The sheriff thinks a woman might have been kidnapped last night, and it's possible Gertrude knows something about it."

Her eyes widened. "Sure, let me see if she's in yet."

Sarah typed something into her computer. "She didn't check in, but she often sneaks in without telling me. You can go on back if you want."

I rushed down the hallway. At her door, I knocked and blew out a breath when she answered. When I entered, Gertrude was watering her plants. "Glinda, did you come about the young woman?"

I wouldn't say Diana was particularly young, but to someone close to ninety, maybe she was. "I'm here about Diana Upton."

Gertrude set down her watering can and took a seat in the hard-backed chair. "Please sit."

I did as she requested. "What do you know?"

"I didn't have a vision of a pink aura, if that's what you're asking, but I had a sense this dog woman is in trouble."

That was what I feared. "Do you know where Diana is?"

"If I did, I would have called the sheriff."

That made sense. "Is there anything you think I can do?"

"Do what you do best."

I almost moaned out loud. Not that tired refrain again. "I'll try."

After we chatted a bit, I thanked her and left. Steve had said to tell him anything that I learned, but revealing that a psychic told me that Diana was in danger wouldn't have helped. Steve and Nash already knew that.

As I walked out, I looked toward the park. If someone had taken Diana, it might have been the same person who stole the dogs. Because people are creatures of habit, he had parked in the same spot as before. I realized nothing would probably come of me searching the area, but I had to do something. If that unruly man harmed Diana, and I didn't try to help, the guilt would eat me alive.

For the next two hours, I scoured the park, but saw no one who looked suspicious or found any evidence of that white van. Even if I stopped over at the sheriff's department and asked if there had been any news, I doubt either man would have told me.

The best thing for me to do was check on Penny and then get ready for tonight's battle between Maude and Miriam.

Chapter Sixteen

I'D BEEN TO the last few parties that the Daniel sisters had thrown, and they always pulled out all the stops, which was why I expected nothing less tonight.

The first party started at the Bubbling Cauldron Coffee Shop and ran from seven to eight. Afterward, people were to head on over to Maude's tea shop party across the street from eight to nine. While the twins pretended as if the celebration was merely a thank you to the community that supported them, everyone knew it was a competition between the Daniel sisters. The only thing missing was a ballot at the end of the night for us to vote for who put on the best show. Even looking back, I couldn't have decided. Both had an amazing spread of drinks, sandwiches, and desserts.

I had to admit that it was hard to paint on a happy face when a woman and two dogs were missing, but I was a Goodall, and Goodall's persevered. Iggy had wanted to come, but I was certain very few people would have appreciated a pink iguana running around a party full of food.

When I arrived at Miriam's shop at ten after seven, it was quite crowded. She had a coffee tasting station that was to die for, in part because she had more toppings than any ice cream shop could dream of having. Her selection ranged from whipped cream to drizzled chocolate, though she had a container of butterscotch syrup for those who swung that way, as well as a bowl of cinnamon. My choice would be chocolate every time.

Her options extended to more than plain coffee. One could have an expresso, a Cuban coffee, or a regular blend that varied from decaf to a high-octane brew.

With my coffee choice in hand, I moved over to the main counter where she had a huge assortment of sandwiches and desserts.

"Isn't this amazing?" Pearl said, sneaking up next to me.

"It is. I can't imagine how Maude can outdo this." Most people preferred coffee to tea, which would put Maude slightly behind her sister. Last year, Maude opened first. Now it was reversed. Being full, I worried that not everyone would walk across the street after the hour was over.

"Any news on locating the dogs or on finding the trainer?" I asked, hoping one of the gossip queens would come through for me.

Pearl shook her head. "Steve and Nash are working around the clock, but they keep coming up empty-handed." She leaned close. "Did you know that Warren Wilson has a record?"

Warren owned the Whippet named Tinkerbell. "No, I didn't. Does the sheriff suspect him of foul play?"

She sipped her Cuban coffee. "I wish I knew. Steve suspects I might be leaking information, so he's watching what he says around me."

Poor Pearl. She looked so distraught. "Surely, that allegation is totally unfounded." I worked very hard to keep a straight face.

"Oh, Glinda. You know as well as I that I can no more keep information to myself than I could dance the jig."

Did anyone do that dance anymore? From what I recalled, it looked like the dancer just shuffled his feet across the floor to a catchy tune. "That sounds like me." I looked around. "Is Steve or Nash coming to the party?"

"They will if they can. I've been hyping it all week."

This would be the first time either of them had experienced anything like this. Before I could ask any more questions, my aunt showed up and whisked Pearl off, hopefully to discuss the latest gossip.

When the hour was up, Miriam shushed everyone while tapping a glass to get the crowds' attention. "I want to thank all of the marvelous people here who have visited my establishment. Seven years is a long time to run a business, but I've had such a wonderful time interacting with you all."

I swear that when she wiped a finger under her eye, it was to remove a fake tear. The crowd clapped, clearly buying her story.

Everyone knew the drill. This event was over. En masse, we walked across the street, which stopped traffic for almost five minutes. I was happy that so many were willing to continue. When I entered the tea shop, I was stunned. Not only was the place decorated with festive balloons, she had a very handsome guitar player singing a love song. I had to hand it to Maude. She knew how to sway the crowd to her side. I really needed to suggest to the town council that there be judges next year.

I managed to get a cup of my favorite tea just as Jaxson

showed up. "Hey, how did Miriam's party go?" he asked.

Jaxson usually wasn't interested in gossip, but I told him my impression. "I have to say that Maude might have won this year. The balloons, the food, and especially the guitar player are a nice touch."

"It looks impressive. I'm going to try some tea and take advantage of those pastries."

"She is a great cook," I said.

At eight-thirty, Steve came in but without his sidekick. Since I was talking with Jaxson at the time about Steve's surprise visit last night, along with Penny's issues with Sam, I didn't think it would be polite to leave Jaxson just to talk to him.

It was near to closing when Steve came over to us. "Glinda, I think you have someone who wants your attention." He was half smiling when he turned around and pointed to Iggy and Aimee who were at the door.

"Oh, my." Iggy was doing circles, and Aimee was meowing. I turned back to Jaxson. "Excuse me."

"I'm coming with you," Jaxson said.

Even though he hadn't been in town for long, he understood Iggy's capabilities, probably because his brother was a believer. He also knew my familiar wouldn't just wander over to check out what was going on, especially after I explained that he wouldn't be welcome.

I'm sure Steve thought my concerned reaction odd, but I didn't have time to explain it to him.

I went outside and picked up my iguana. "What are you doing here?" I tried to hide my worry.

"I found Snookums," Iggy said lifting his head.

"*We* found Snookums," Aimee added.

"You did?" I didn't need them to argue. I told Jaxson what they said. I faced my little sources once more. "Where did you find him?"

"He was huddled outside between the Tiki Hut and your parents' place. He didn't look so good, so we invited him inside where we gave him some water. He told us where he'd been and how he'd escaped."

Several questions bombarded me. "Snookums can talk?"

"Yes. He told us that he's Patty O'Neal's familiar."

Oh, this made all the difference in the world. I looked back at Jaxson. "Can you get the sheriff. Tell him I know where the dogs are."

"You do?"

"Yes. Iggy and Aimee just told me. Kind of."

He held up a hand, clearly not understanding all of it, but he did as I asked and rushed inside. It took the sheriff at least a minute before Jaxson escorted him out.

"What's this I hear about you knowing where the dogs are?"

It was time to tell him the truth—just as soon as I laid my eyes on this missing animal. "He's in the stairwell near my apartment."

"Let's go."

All we had to do was cross the parking lot, and we were at the restaurant. Instead of walking around and entering by the side entrance, we went through the front. Aunt Fern was still at Maude's party. Bertie Sidwell, her replacement was at the cash register. Considering we only had three tables occupied, Aunt Fern probably should have shut down for the night. She never would have though, because then the clients probably would have gone over to Dolly's diner—something she would not stand for.

"Where is he?" I asked Iggy.

"Under the stairs."

"You should have taken him into the apartment to keep him safe." If someone took him the first time, this person could have returned, but what was done was done.

"He was too tired to climb the stairs, and I couldn't carry him."

"Good point."

Sure enough, Snookums was there. He was dirty and looked exhausted. I set Iggy down and then squatted in front of the dog. "Hi there, Snookums. Can you tell me what happened?"

He looked up at the sheriff and then back at me. "Can you trust him?"

That was an odd question. "Yes. Completely, but only I can hear you."

"That's good to know." He told me a tale that was hard to believe.

"Let me relay to the sheriff and to my friend what you told me."

"Okay, but I'm really hungry. Do you have any food?"

I looked up at Jaxson. "Do you think you can go into the kitchen and let the chef know that we have a really hungry dog out here? See if he can spare a bone or something?"

"Sure."

As soon as he left, Steve glanced at the dog and then at me. "I'm not going to ask how you can understand him, but what did he say?"

"A man abducted him from the park, or rather Snookums followed the man. Looking back, he thinks he might have been drugged or something since he only blindly obeys Patty."

"What happened after he followed the man?"

"The guy put him in his van and then took off."

"I don't suppose this pooch knows the color or model of this van?"

I had no idea. I looked over at Snookums, who appeared ready to drop. Poor dear. "Do you remember anything?"

"I'm not blind. It was a white van, but I didn't get the license plate number. As I said, it was like I was in a trance and couldn't stop myself from doing what he asked."

I looked up at Steve. "It was a white van."

"Seriously?"

I understood his skepticism. I was lucky. I've had Iggy for so long that a smart and verbal animal no longer seemed odd. "Yes. Just like the one that Silas Adams saw."

"Well, I'll be. Can he describe the man?"

"The man looked like every other guy. Not too tall, not too old, but he had scraggly brown hair."

Aha. Ten bucks said it was the man in the diner with Diana. I told my thoughts to Steve anyway. He then put the information into his phone.

"That's great. I realize that since this wonder dog is not from Witch's Cove, he won't be familiar with the roads, but can he tell us how long they traveled?"

"I'm not a dog person, but I don't think dogs have a good sense of time."

"I do too," Snookums said, acting offended.

I told Steve his response.

"That's good to know." From the way he was tilting his head, Steve wanted to believe him. "Does Snookums know where he was taken?"

I looked back at the dog. He lowered his head. "Not exactly."

"What do you mean by not exactly." I worked hard not to let my frustration color my tone.

Jaxson rushed over with a bowl of something. "The cook ground up some raw meat. He said dogs love steak."

Snookums looked up. "Boy, do I."

As soon as Jaxson placed the bowl on the floor, Snookums went to town on the food. "Could you get him some more water?" I hated to ask, but I needed to be there with the dog.

"Sure."

I was happy Jaxson didn't balk. Once Snookums ate half of his food, he looked up.

"I remember seeing a very worn sign on the side of the barn before I was *escorted* inside," the dog said.

"Do you remember anything about the sign?" I asked. Most signs on the sides of barns were ads for either national chains or local establishments.

"It said Spellbound something. I couldn't see the second word because the paint was so faded."

I looked over at Steve and smiled. I knew that barn. Back when I was growing up, the sign was new. It read Spellbound Diner. Jaxson returned with a bowl of water and placed it on the floor. "What did I miss?" he asked.

"I believe I know where Snookums spent the last few days."

"Where?" he asked.

"Do you remember the old barn off State Road 25? It had a white picket fence around the property. Back in the day, it was a cattle farm. I think it's now abandoned."

"Sure, I do. Did my fair share of drinking around there."

Great. Letting the sheriff know he'd been a delinquent wasn't smart, but I doubt Steve would hold it against him now.

"That's where this guy took Snookums," I said.

"I need a time out here, Glinda," Steve said. "Just to be sure, you're not just yanking my chain about this animal being able to talk, are you?"

"No." His comment was almost insulting.

Chapter Seventeen

AFTER STEVE SAW me chat with Iggy and then with Snookums, he was only now asking me if I could communicate with them? I could lie and say that I couldn't, but it would be a lot easier if I were honest with him. In the future, if Iggy told me something important, I wanted Steve to believe me. "I can communicate with some animals."

"Some, but not all?"

I did a brief explanation of what a familiar was.

"It's a witch thing then?" he asked.

Steve was struggling, but I appreciated he wanted to understand. "Yes, it is."

Iggy sat up. "I can show him. Ask him to write down a number while you keep your back turned, and then have him show it only to me. I'll tell you, and then you tell Steve. He has to believe you then."

"That is brilliant." I faced Steve. I told him Iggy's suggestion.

"Seriously? Your pink iguana can read?"

I held up a hand to Iggy. I didn't need to hear his indignation. "Yes, Iggy can read, and clearly Snookums can too. He just told you what was on the side of the barn."

"Fine. Seeing is believing."

My first instinct was to tell him to leave, but I swallowed my pride. "Go ahead and show Iggy the number."

With my back turned, I listened for the rustling of paper, but I heard nothing. Most likely, Steve was typing something on his phone or holding up fingers. Either way would work.

Iggy told me the number was four.

"The number is four," I said before facing Steve.

"I don't believe it." He sounded dumbfounded.

I spun around, and Jaxson chuckled. "You'll get used to it," he said. "Glinda has many talents. I struggled at first too, but now I take it in stride."

Steve inhaled and let out a long slow breath. "Good to know."

Enough of this proof stuff. "Now that I've established Iggy, Aimee, and Snookums can speak, are we going to rescue Mittens or not?"

"There is no *we*, Glinda. This could be dangerous. If the man who took the dogs is the same guy you saw in the diner, he might have Diana. Though I would like Jaxson to come with me, if he doesn't mind, to show us where this barn is located. You need to stay here."

I loved that he was trying to be Mr. Protective and all, but that wouldn't work for me. "You need me to be able to talk to Snookums. He might be able to tell you the layout of the barn or even identify the man."

His jaw tightened, and he didn't answer for a few seconds. "Fine."

Satisfaction filled me. "Why don't you call Nash and ask him to help out." I was worried that if this dog thief stooped so low as to steal dogs—probably with the intention of selling them—he might own a gun to protect his investment. "There might be more than one person involved."

"You're right," Snookums said. "There are two."

I stepped over to the dog. "What can you tell me about this other person?"

"It's Diana, the trainer lady. She's helping him."

I swiveled to face both men. "Snookums just told me that Diana Upton is in on this dognapping."

"Seriously?" Steve asked.

I didn't know what else I could do to convince him that I was on the up and up.

He held up a hand. "Okay. I'm calling Nash. How about you and Snookums ride with me while Nash goes with Jaxson? Once we know what we're up against, you need to move into Jaxson's car. Nash and I will make the arrests."

There wouldn't be room in the cruiser for all of us. "Works for me."

Steve texted Nash, who took all of two minutes to get there. "What's up?" Nash asked.

"Jaxson will fill you in on the way. This here is Snookums, Patty O'Neal's dog. He can communicate with Glinda." Steve looked over at Snookums. "You up for this?"

Snookums barked, clearly understanding that was the only way to communicate with a non-witch.

"That means yes," I said, feeling full of myself.

"Where are we going?" Nash asked Steve.

"We're heading to a farm off of State Road 25, where hopefully we'll be rescuing another dog or two and arresting a few people—including Diana Upton."

Since Snookums only weighed about six pounds, I picked

him up. I figured he'd had enough walking for a lifetime. I still couldn't believe this tiny animal could walk or run all the way from the barn to town. He was a super dog for sure. "Was Mittens with you in the barn?" I asked.

"Yes, and several other dogs were too."

"Do you have any idea why they took you? Was it to sell you?"

"You don't want to know. It's embarrassing."

"You can tell me on the way," I said.

"What did he say?" Steve asked.

I relayed the information. I could almost feel Steve's respect for me growing.

"Oh, I just remembered something," Snookums said. "I heard Diana call the guy Phil."

That was great information. I told Steve and Nash what Snookums said.

"Okay. Phil it is," Steve said.

Naturally, Nash looked even more confused. "You believe that Glinda can talk to a dog?"

We didn't have time to go through the proof again. "Yes. Ask Jaxson," I said. "Steve will confirm it too. I'm guessing you didn't come across anyone by the name of Phil when you were searching for other missing dogs?"

"No."

"We'll sort this all out on the drive over," Steve said.

I had no doubt that I was going to have some trouble with Aimee and Iggy when I asked them to stay back since both would want to come. Iggy, especially, loved being in the thick of things, but I feared that those two might get in the way. "It's probably too dangerous for Aimee to go," I told Iggy.

"You're small and can hide unnoticed, but Aimee isn't as flexible." Besides, Iggy could cloak himself, at least for short periods of time.

"I get it. That's code for asking me to keep her safe."

"Exactly. When I get back, I'll ask Aunt Fern for an extra helping of hibiscus flowers for you."

He stuck his tongue out at me. "I appreciate it. But don't let anything bad happen to you."

Iggy usually wasn't this protective. Most likely, he was showing off for his cat girlfriend. "Would you miss me if something did happen?"

He glanced away for a moment. "You know I would."

I flashed him a quick smile. "Good to know."

Once outside, we piled into two cars, ready to take down this ring of dog thieves. I'd be lying if I said I wasn't nervous. While I was merely translating what Snookums told me, what if he was making it up? It was possible he'd run off to explore and needed some excuse for leaving. When the sun went down, he might not have been able to find his way home. Uncertain what to do, he laid low for a while until he made his way back to Witch's Cove.

In case he was telling the truth, I gave Steve directions. The next turn wouldn't be for a while. "Snookums, can you tell me how you managed to escape?"

His answer would help me decide if he really had been taken. The fact Mittens was also missing made me lean in the direction of him telling the truth.

"The man, Phil, took me out of my cage and set me down so I could do my male prowess thing with this cute little female Papillon. While I was busy sniffing around, Phil

153

removed another dog from his cage. That's when I realized I could escape unnoticed—at least for long enough to get out. Remember, ducking under cages and running around obstacles is what I do."

"That's true. Wasn't the barn locked up tight?" I asked.

"Not that time. Phil must have had a lot on his mind, because before he let me out, he'd gone out back carrying a shovel. That's when I slipped out and ran."

"What did he say?" Steve asked.

Once more I relayed the information.

"A shovel?" Steve asked.

"That's what Snookums said." I turned back to the dog. "Do you know what he was digging?" I asked.

"No. When I ran off, Phil was about ten feet into the woods, but I didn't wait around to see what he was up to."

"Interesting." I had no idea what to think about that. Okay, I had an idea, but I didn't want to go there. I told Steve.

He said nothing for a bit. "If this Phil and Diana were partners, I wonder where she was in all of this?" Steve said. "If the two of them are working together, they might have left the diner and gone straight to the barn."

That would explain why her stuff was still in her hotel room. "Or he killed her," I said. "Remember, she wanted a bigger cut of the operation."

Steve whistled. "I hope you are wrong."

"Me too."

He looked over at Snookums. "Could you describe the layout of the barn for me?"

"I didn't see all of it since he kept us on a tight leash. We were only able to get out when it was time to breed."

"Yikes. Is that why he took you? To impregnate the other dogs?" I asked.

"I wasn't able to ask him directly, but that was my guess."

I repeated the answer to Steve.

"Dogs at this level would sell for a lot of money," Steve said.

I shivered at that thought. "Back to the layout," I said. "Was it one big room?"

"No, I saw Phil go into another part of the barn."

I relayed what he'd said to Steve.

"Thanks, Snookums. That helps," he said.

I stroked Snookums' back. "Since you're not from around here, how were you able to find Witch's Cove?"

He looked up at me with his big brown eyes. "I might not know exactly where your town is located, but since it is a beach town, I followed the sun as it set. That's where the beach would be. It took me two days to get there."

"Wow. I'm impressed. Following the sun was smart."

"Yup," he said.

Too bad Snookums would be leaving town once he was reunited with Patty. I bet he and Iggy could have been good friends since they seemed to possess the same temperament— determined and stubborn.

Jaxson, who was driving the car behind us, honked, and I realized we'd arrived at the start of the white picket fence. I needed to pay better attention. "Turn right. Here."

Steve executed the turn flawlessly but then looked over at me. "A little more notice next time?" Thankfully, he didn't sound angry.

"I will. I'm a little nervous, that's all."

"I understand. How much farther?" he asked.

"A couple hundred feet ahead is the entrance. Turn in there. The roof on the main house has collapsed, but the barn used to be in fairly good condition. I haven't been out this way in quite a long time."

He pulled to a stop because the gate was closed. "Hey, Snookums, did you notice any security cameras inside the barn?" Steve asked.

"No, but that doesn't mean there weren't any. I was kind of too scared to take notice," he said.

Once more I translated.

Steve exited the car, opened the gate, and then pulled in. He cut the engine about a hundred feet from the white van that was parked next to the barn. This had to be the place. Jaxson stopped behind us.

"Nash and I will take it from here. Please escort Mr. Snookums to Jaxson's car. And thanks for your help."

"Sure." I was quite happy to sit this one out.

It was pitch black, which hopefully would prevent Phil and Diana from spotting them. Steve looked over at me, clearly waiting for me to do as he asked.

"I'm going." With Snookums in my arms, I moved over to Jaxson's car, but both he and Nash had already gotten out.

"Do you guys need me as backup?" Jaxson asked Steve. "I'm quite handy in a fight, as long as there are no weapons involved."

"Not right now, but be ready to take chase in case Phil gets the slip on us. I don't want Glinda to be alone."

I wasn't alone. I had a six-pound fearless dog with me.

"Can do."

Jaxson got back into the car and started the engine. He probably wanted to be ready in case they had another vehicle hidden somewhere should they need to make a run for it. Since it was very sticky outside, I appreciated the cool air.

"Do you trust Snookums?" Jaxson asked.

I wasn't sure why he asked, but I answered anyway. "I do."

Jaxson nodded. "Then I do too."

I kept petting the dog, partially to halt the worry that was inching its way up my spine. What if this Phil guy got the drop on both Steve and Nash?

I understood that it would take them a few minutes to walk to the barn, but once there, how hard would it be to arrest the two of them? What if there were more people inside, and Steve and Nash were captured too? Or worse, shot?

My nerves were out of control. "Snookums, did anyone else show up to the barn while you were there?"

"Once. I think he was a vet. Phil wanted him to check out one of the dogs. I could tell the doc didn't want to be there."

Phil might have threatened the poor man's family if he didn't come. I told Jaxson what he said.

"Phil's evening forest digging is troubling," Jaxson said. "Does he know what Phil was burying?"

"I already asked him. He doesn't know, but it's possible the sick dog might have died, and he was burying him."

"Maybe, or he killed Diana," Jaxson said.

"That's gruesome." But it was what I thought too.

"I agree." He looked over at me. "Do you think there is a spell you could put on me so I could understand Iggy, Aimee, and any other familiar?" Jaxson asked.

Wow. That question floored me. While Jaxson had been very helpful, in the back of my head, I thought he kind of believed I was just a bit crazy. I wanted to take his request seriously though. "I don't know. I wouldn't trust me to do the spell. You know what happened the last time."

"That wasn't your fault. How were you to know Hazel mixed up the ingredients? It kind of turned out okay in the end though, didn't it?"

I chuckled. "If you call being able to see ghosts okay, then yes. Iggy wasn't all that happy, but I think he's come to grips with it."

Jaxson placed a hand on my wrist. "I see something."

"Is it Steve and Nash?"

"I think so."

The two men emerged from the darkness with a man in front of them. Behind them was a barking Border Collie. Josh Randall would be so excited to learn his precious Mittens was okay.

"What about the other dogs?" Snookums asked.

"I'm sure the sheriff will make arrangements for them to be taken someplace safe. Their owners must be frantic. Can any of the other dogs communicate like you?"

"Not that I know of. Phil didn't give us a lot of play time, so it's possible."

I chuckled, happy this mess was almost over. "Where is Diana?" I asked.

"Good question."

Nash loaded the offender, who was in cuffs, into the back seat of the cruiser. He slipped into the front seat while Steve walked over to us.

Jaxson rolled down the window, and Steve leaned in. "Glinda, once more I apologize for underestimating you. Without your and Snookums' help, these dogs would have never been reunited with their owners."

"You're welcome, but where's Diana? I thought she'd be with Phil."

"I asked him, but he said he didn't know."

"Do you believe him?" I asked.

"Not at all."

Steve called to Mittens, who pranced over, seemingly excited to be free. Jaxson slipped out and opened the back door, motioning for Mittens to get in. He must have smelled Snookums, because he hopped in and then placed his paws on the back of the front seat. He then barked.

"Someone is happy to see you," I said to Snookums.

"I'm glad to see him too. Can you put me in the back?"

"Sure."

I placed him next to Mittens. The two dogs immediately sniffed and then licked each other. When I faced forward, the moon peeked out from the clouds and shone on something pink next to the van. I pushed open my door.

"Glinda, where are you going?" Jaxson asked.

"It's okay, I need to check something out." Phil was in custody, and I was sure Steve and Nash made sure no one else was inside.

Steve was next to me in a flash. "What are you doing?" he asked.

"I saw something pink."

"Where?"

"Next to the van."

For once, Steve didn't argue with me. I trotted over, and he followed. Sure enough, on the ground was a pink and white bandana. I pointed to it instead of picking it up. "That belongs to Diana. She always wore it."

"I'll be. How about grabbing Snookums? I could use his help with something."

I wasn't sure what he was up to, but I was happy to oblige. "Sure."

I returned to Jaxson's car and told him what I'd found. "I'm sure it belongs to Diana."

"Phil must have been burying her body," Jaxson said.

Shivers shot down my spine. "We're about to find out, assuming Snookums can remember where he saw Phil digging. Can you stay here with Mittens?"

"I can."

He was the best. With Snookums in tow, I returned to Steve. Between him searching the woods using his flashlight and Snookums giving directions, Steve found the shallow grave in no time.

He turned toward me. "How about taking Snookums back to the car?"

As curious as I was, I didn't need to see a dead body. The clues all pointed to this being Diana Upton. "Happy to."

I slid into the car with Jaxson and told him about the grave.

"Was it Diana's?"

"I didn't wait around long enough to see."

"Smart," he said.

We said little until Steve returned from the back. He

replaced the shovel in his trunk and then came over. Jaxson rolled down the window.

"It was Diana. I've called the coroner. Because it's late, I asked Sheriff Misty Willows from over in Liberty if she could assist. It has become very clear that Witch's Cove needs more help."

"No kidding. What about the other dogs? What's going to happen to them?"

"I've called a rescue center. They, along with their vet, will arrive shortly to check them out. The dogs will be returned to their sanctuary. Hopefully, we'll be able to find all of the owners in due time."

"That's great. Have you called Patty O'Neal and Josh Randall yet?" I asked.

"I was about too. Can you take both dogs to the station? I'll have the two owners meet you there."

"Great."

Steve walked back to his cruiser. He should have looked triumphant, but instead, he appeared to be exhausted. I could understand. Now that the adrenaline rush was leaving my body, I wanted to crash.

As soon as Steve started his cruiser, we took off, ready to reunite the dogs with their owners.

Chapter Eighteen

W HEN WE ARRIVED at the station, two vehicles were parked in front, and both car doors opened at the same time. Josh Randall exited one, while Patty and her whole family slipped out of the other. I jumped out and opened the back door to let the reunion begin.

Mittens was big enough to leap down, but to avoid Snookums from injuring himself, I lifted him up and set him onto the pavement. As the dogs raced to their owners, everyone's squeals made my heart sing. Josh dropped to his knees and hugged Mittens so hard, I thought he'd crush the dog. Never in a million years did I expect Mr. Randall to cry. He might not be the best with humans, but he did seem to have a great bond with his dog.

Patty came over carrying Snookums, smiling and laughing. "Thank you so much for rescuing him."

"Actually, Snookums rescued himself. He led us to the other dogs." I ran a hand over his head. "You have a very brave dog," I told her.

She brought the back of his head to her lips and kissed him. "He is the best. Can you tell us what happened?"

"Let's go inside. The sheriff will be here momentarily, and I'll let him fill everyone in all at the same time. I'm sure Mr.

Randall has a lot of questions too."

I also was curious what went down inside the barn and how the other dogs looked.

We hadn't even reached the front entrance before Steve's cruiser pulled up and parked in front of the building. A moment later, both of them had opened the back doors and helped Phil out of the car. After Nash led him inside, everyone followed.

As Nash escorted Phil directly to a holding cell, Steve faced us all. "It's been a long night, but I'm sure you have questions. Let me begin by saying I'm sorry this happened. Phil Thomas stole a lot of dogs. He was breeding them in order to sell them for an obscene profit."

Mr. Randall as well as Patty O'Neal gasped. "He needs to be punished," Randall said.

"He will be," Steve said. "Not only did he steal many dogs, he allegedly murdered Diana Upton. According to sources, he and Diana were in this together. She got a little greedy, and he killed her."

I couldn't believe Steve was jumping to conclusions without proof, but I totally agreed with him.

The chatter intensified. "Did he drug my Snookums?" Patty asked. "He knows better than to follow strangers."

"No. According to Phil, Diana paid a witch to put a spell on the dogs that basically hypnotized them. They did whatever he asked."

I was right, but it didn't bring as much joy as I thought it would. I had to give Steve credit for believing a witch could do this. While I was certain the two owners had a ton of questions, I only had one. "Did Phil give you the name of this witch?" I asked unable to stop myself from butting in. The witch needed to be punished too.

"Phil was a bit tight-lipped about that. He claimed he didn't know much other than Diana called her Daphne."

"Does this Daphne live in Witch's Cove?" I asked.

"That's all Phil seemed to know," Steve said.

"Was Mittens mistreated in any way?" Josh Randall asked.

"Not that I could tell. A rescue center team should be at the barn by now to check out the other dogs, but I suggest you get your dog looked at too."

Snookums looked up at Patty. "I'm fine. I promise."

"I'll for sure have our vet look over my dog."

"We had a contestant in the show by the name of Brad Thomas, who had a Golden Retriever," Mr. Randall asked. "Was he related to this Phil Thomas?"

"We're not sure, Mr. Randall. In the morning, I plan to check it out."

Josh sniffled and then lifted his head. "How did you find them?"

I thought Steve would ask me to explain, but he did a fine job of coming up with a story that didn't include me talking to animals. In fact, he avoided mentioning anything about Snookums telling us where he'd been held. That would have resulted in too many questions. Instead, he said he had a source that had seen a man load some animals into an unused barn.

"No matter how you did it," Mr. Randall said. "Thank you."

I was happy he didn't ask why I was involved.

"If you'll excuse me. I need to tend to Mittens," he said.

"He looks emaciated."

No, he didn't, but Mr. Randall probably just needed an excuse to leave. Since everything seemed to be taken care of, Jaxson and I slipped out too. "I know you have an early shift tomorrow," Jaxson said, "but how about some ice cream with chocolate sauce and sprinkles. I need to deplane, so to speak."

I laughed. "I didn't picture you as a sprinkles kind of guy."

He smiled. "There is a lot you don't know about me."

That sounded intriguing, but I didn't think it would be wise to delve into that. "It's late. I believe the ice cream shop is closed."

"It is, but Drake not only has a wine cooler, there is a refrigerator in his office. Naturally, we store ice cream in there."

I smiled. "You guys are full of surprises." I didn't want to spoil the surprise by saying Drake and I had indulged in many ice cream parties in the past.

All he had to do was pull the car across the street and park. Instead of entering through the front, we cut through the back alley to the beachside entrance. To my surprise, Drake was still in his office doing paperwork.

Drake looked up. "Hey, what are you two doing here?"

"It's a long story. I promised Glinda an ice cream extravaganza to celebrate the taking down of our two notorious dog thieves."

Drake's eyes widened. "You found the dogs?"

"We did," I said. "One of the dogs, who is a familiar, told us where the rest of the dogs were being held. But first, I'm making a very decadent bowl of ice cream. Then we will regale you with our tale of heroics." I smiled.

Drake laughed as he closed his laptop. "I can't wait."

Jaxson pulled the ice cream out of the freezer while Drake located the toppings. I retrieved the dishes from one of the cabinets. In no time, we had three ice cream masterpieces done.

Drake cleaned off a portion of his desk and we chose our spot. "Tell me everything," Drake said.

I began with Iggy and Aimee showing up at Maude's party, and then Steve, Jaxson, and I returning to the Tiki Hut to ask Snookums what happened.

"I'm sorry I missed that. What did Steve think of your ability to communicate with animals? Or doesn't he believe you?" Drake asked.

"I got this," Jaxson said. He detailed Iggy's *pick a number trick*. "It worked like a charm. Steve was onboard after that."

"I'm happy for you, Glinda. It will make interacting with him in the future a lot easier."

"I hope so."

Drake stirred his ice cream, making swirls of chocolate in a now soupy mess. "This familiar was able to direct you where he had been held? I'm surprised he knew the roads."

"He didn't know anything other than he remembered the faded Spellbound Diner sign painted on the side of the barn."

Drake pointed a finger at Jaxson. "I know that place. If I recall, you got busted for drinking at that farm."

Jaxson laughed. "Yeah, but that was the old me."

I didn't want to talk about his bad boy days—at least not now. "Regardless of his history with the place, Jaxson and I were in charge of watching Snookums while Steve and Nash did the whole rescue thing. The man who was breeding these animals was in cahoots with the trainer."

"It didn't end well for her though," Jaxson said. "Phil killed her, or so we believe." He explained how Snookums saw Phil digging a grave.

"Ouch," Drake shot back. "Sounds like a slam dunk case to me."

I then explained how Diana had hired a witch to put a spell on the dogs. "This hypnotic spell was what created the pink aura."

"Do you know who this witch is?" Drake asked.

"Her name is Daphne. No last name. I figure if she created something that strong, she must be really powerful."

"But…you hate loose ends," Jaxson said.

I understood what he was getting at. "Are you asking if I plan to pursue her?" I did appreciate his protective side.

"That is exactly what I'm asking." I swear his eyes darkened or else the overhead lights had dimmed.

"What if I said yes?" I wouldn't. Even if it did, I could never prove anything anyway. Regardless of whether I was satisfied, no court would convict her.

On the other hand, if at some point, I happened to run into Gertrude or maybe Jack Hanson, I might ask them if they knew of a witch named Daphne.

"I'd try to talk you out of it. This witch is dangerous."

"I know, but that won't stop me from asking around." I was only teasing, curious how he'd react.

"Glinda." Jaxson was losing patience. "I have a better idea."

"What? Let you try to find her?" I was enjoying this.

"No." He faced his brother. "I love working with you, bro, but I need more in my life."

Whoa. Where had that come from? He wasn't leaving town because I might ask about a fellow witch, was he?

"I know," Drake said. "What's your plan, assuming you have one?"

My gaze bounced between the brothers until Jaxson's gaze locked onto mine. "It depends on Glinda."

"Me?" What was he talking about? My mind couldn't even fathom what I had to do with anything.

"I think Glinda should open an investigation firm with me as her partner."

My mouth dropped open. "Say what?"

He chuckled. "Is your surprise due to the idea of opening your own firm, or having me as your partner? Remember, I'm the muscle."

He was more than just the muscle. "I have a full-time job."

Drake reached out and clasped my hand. "You do, but that hasn't ever stopped you from snooping. You did find out who killed Cliff Duncan, who shot Morgan Oliver, and who had stolen two—or in this case more—dogs."

"What are you suggesting?" My heart was beating so fast, I could barely form any words. In my dreams, I imagined myself being this crime fighting superhero. I never pursued it because I had no intention of dealing with any kind of violence. My reality was taking food orders and talking to people.

"For starters, cut down on your hours," Drake suggested.

"I suppose I could do that. Aunt Fern did say that if I ever wanted to pursue another career that she'd let me go."

Both Jaxson and Drake smiled. "There you go," Jaxson said.

"There's one major problem."

"What's that?" Jaxson asked.

"I'm not a private investigator." I had actually done some research to see what it would take. The first step involved taking courses at a school that was several hours away. "It would take at least a minimum of a year to get my license, assuming Steve would sign off on the hours I've spent helping him out."

"Who said anything about being a private investigator?" Jaxson asked.

He wasn't making much sense. "I can't hang out a shingle without one."

"Sure, you can. You can be an amateur sleuth, just like you are now. You'll have to turn over all dangerous information to Steve and Nash, but that is what you already do."

I scraped my spoon along the sides of the bowl to gather the remains of chocolate sauce, hoping it would calm me. I looked up at Jaxson. "I never pictured you as a dreamer. We'd be lucky to get one case a month. I couldn't afford to pay for groceries or gas—or you—assuming anyone would pay."

"With your track record and connections? They'd be foolish not to. If the case is small, I wouldn't be surprised if Steve or Nash refers you," Jaxson said. "Besides, I've saved up quite a chunk of change from when I worked at the tech company. I'd work for free in the beginning. If we don't have a heavy load, I'll pick up hours with Drake."

"Wow. That is generous of you."

"Don't forget you have Iggy," Drake added. "He can talk to other familiars, which will bring more value to the table."

I laughed. "You guys are serious, aren't you?"

Jaxson scooped out more ice cream. "Deadly serious. All I ask is that you think about it. We could have our office hours three days a week, and then work our other jobs the other three or four days. You get off work at three. That gives people time to find you."

He was making it sound so appealing. It would give my never-ending curiosity a good reason to stick my nose into other people's business. "I'll think about it."

Aunt Fern would be supportive. My mother and father would say I was a little crazy, but they'd understand. Eventually. As for the law enforcement in town? I had a feeling Steve would think I'd interfere too much and that I might hurt his chances of finding a real criminal. If I promised not to have anything to do with the big cases, unless he asked me to, then he might be okay with it.

I yawned. "I think I need to talk this over with Iggy and Aunt Fern. I appreciate both of your support."

Jaxson leaned back in his chair. "What should we call our firm? Goodall and Harrison?"

I laughed, thankful my name came first in the alphabet. "You do realize that Iggy will want to be named too."

"By all means."

While I truly didn't think this would work, I wanted to clear up one more thing. "I'd need an office, and office space in this town is expensive!"

Drake pointed a finger at me. "I have that covered. Howl At the Moon is two stories. I mostly keep baskets, old wine crates, and other stuff upstairs that I tell myself I'll repurpose someday to make bookcases or coffee tables out of. I could move the junk off to the side, and you could set up a small office there," Drake said.

"There's an outside staircase too," Jaxson added.

I couldn't help but wonder if the stars were all aligning. I pushed back my chair. "I can't tell you how much I adore the both of you. Thank you."

"No thanks needed," Drake said. "All of your crazy theories bring lightness to our lives."

That made me laugh. I stood. "Thanks for your help, Jaxson."

"Anytime."

Chapter Nineteen

THE NEXT DAY at work, I gave Penny a brief rundown about what happened with the dogs.

"What about the other animals?" she asked. "The ones that Phil stole before?"

"I don't know yet, but Steve asked for help from Animal Services and said they would all be checked out by a vet. Steve and Nash would do what they could to find their owners."

Penny smiled and then hugged me. "You are an amazing person, Glinda Goodall."

"Aw shucks, though if it hadn't been for Iggy and Aimee finding Snookums, those dogs might never have been found."

"I don't believe that."

"Well, thanks." I never considered myself as a real sleuth—just someone who was nosy enough to learn stuff.

I expected Penny to return to her station, but she seemed to freeze. "Don't. Turn. Around. There is the most gorgeous man I've ever seen about to sit in your section."

Penny had just dumped Sam, and yet here she was looking for another to take his place. I glanced over my shoulder and stilled. "That's my father's friend, Hunter Ashwell. He was at my dad's birthday party on Monday."

"You know him? Can you introduce me?"

Was she kidding? "I barely said two words to him. It's my table, but he doesn't know that. Go wait on him."

"Thank you!" Penny rushed off.

Penny, Penny, Penny. She was a work in progress, but I loved her. She, too, made my life a lot more interesting.

At that thought, my stomach soured. If I cut down on my hours, I wouldn't see Penny as often. Or else, when I did work, I could make sure it was on the days Penny was here.

I looked over at her. She was taking Hunter's order and grinning. I hoped the two of them hit it off. Hunter was good looking, had a steady job, and my dad liked him. If they dated, I could ask Hunter about my father and his new strange need to hunt.

Or was it strange? My mom talked to the dead, named her dog Toto, and had a long, yellow runner from the front entrance of their funeral home that led straight to the chapel. She lived her life as if she would always follow the yellow brick road.

My dad was actually the more normal of the two. Though of late, I wasn't so sure.

After Penny finished taking Hunter's order, she just sighed as she rushed past me toward the kitchen. I had another table to attend to, so I hurried off.

I couldn't help but entertain the idea of what it would be like to cut down on my hours and spend my time solving crimes. If money weren't an issue, I'd do it in a heartbeat.

Unfortunately, by the time my shift was over, I was no closer to an answer. Since I hadn't arrived home until close to midnight, it had been too late to talk to Iggy about it— though I could guess what he'd say. He'd give me a resounding yes. If I agreed to start the firm, Iggy would be rather insistent that his name be given top billing. Unless, the person was native to Witch's Cove, they'd write me off as a kook. Too bad. Pink Iguana Sleuths had a nice ring to it.

When I finally went upstairs to my apartment, I was rather tired. Needless to say, I hadn't slept well since my mind had refused to shut off last night.

As soon as I pushed open the door, Iggy jumped down off his stool. "You didn't wake me when you came in last night. What happened with the dogs?"

I probably should have told him. "Let me get a tea, and I will tell you everything."

Once I was settled on the couch, I regaled him with how great Snookums had been in helping us locate the animals.

"I love a happily ever after, but I hope you never plan on doing any kind of animal competition with me. If I ever competed in climbing, jumping, swimming, and racing, I'd be such a star that everyone would try to kidnap me."

I laughed hard. I then patted the sofa seat next to me. "Come here. I have something I need to ask you."

Iggy obliged by climbing up. At some point, I'd have to buy new furniture since his claws were ruining the fabric.

"What is it?" he asked.

I detailed Jaxson's plan about starting my own firm. "What do you think?"

"Are you kidding me? That would be my dream come true, though I have a list of demands."

I smiled. "I'm sure you do, but I haven't decided to do it yet."

"Have you spoken with Aunt Fern?"

"That is what I want to do as soon as she finishes work."

"Wait here," Iggy said, sounding more excited than he ever had—unless I counted his joy when he learned Cliff Duncan had died. That might have been Iggy's happiest day. Sad, right?

Before I could tell him to stop, he was through the cat door. No doubt, he was racing downstairs to tell Aunt Fern to haul herself up the stairs and talk to me. I'm sure he understood she'd need to find someone to man the checkout counter. Most likely he figured she'd do what she needed to.

My iguana was too darn impetuous. Hmm. I wonder where he got that trait?

Ten minutes later, a happy looking iguana jumped back through the cat door, followed by my aunt—not through the cat door but rather through the people door.

"What's this about starting your own detective agency?" Thankfully, my aunt sounded excited.

"I think Iggy might have exaggerated."

"I did not," he shot back.

"Whatever. Did you get someone to cover the front for you?" I asked.

"Yes." Aunt Fern sat down. "Tell me what spurred this on."

I briefly filled her in about finding the dogs. "Afterward, we went over to Drake's store where the three of us had some wonderful ice cream sundaes. Did you know that Jaxson likes more sprinkles on his dessert than I do?"

She clapped. "I am so happy for you."

"About the opportunity to help others or that there is someone out there who likes more sprinkles than me?"

"All of the above, but I'm even more excited that Jaxson is your boyfriend."

"Whoa." I held up my hands to forestall that rumor. I wouldn't be surprised if Iggy made up something to tell her. "We are just friends."

"Uh-huh."

I didn't want to get into this. If I did, Aunt Fern would ask about Steve Rocker, who I admit, held a small place in my heart.

"I need your opinion about opening a business. Drake said I could clean up the second floor above his store and use it as my office."

"Oh, that's wonderful."

"I know, but if I'm not working here, I may not learn the gossip."

My aunt patted my hand. "You can always ask me."

"I know, but at some point, I'll need to develop my own contacts." I realize that my aunt had many more years left in her, but what about Pearl? Or the Daniel sisters? I wasn't convinced that Maude would last another twenty years. As for Dolly? That was a no brainer. She was too stubborn to go down lightly.

"Do what I did when I became of age," she said.

"Which was?"

"I joined a women's entrepreneur group."

Both the Daniel sisters still owned their own business, as did my aunt and Dolly. "Pearl was a business owner?"

"Are you kidding? She owned a bookstore first and then a nursery—for plants not kids. Once her own children were born, she sold it. Made a real nice chunk of change, I might add."

"I never knew."

My aunt smiled. "Our women-in-business group no longer exists, but you can join another group—one that gets together all the time."

I liked the idea, but I couldn't figure out what. "Do you have any suggestions?"

"What about joining a knitting group? From what I've heard, the women meet once a week at Sarah Lipton's store and knit up a storm—and of course, gossip."

"That sounds promising, but I don't knit."

"You could learn," she said.

"I suppose if we lived in an area where scarves, sweaters, and hats were needed, I might consider it."

"Okay. We'll keep it on the table for now." She grinned. "I just heard from Eileen Gibson that her bridge group lost one of their members. You used to play when you were little."

I did love playing cards. "I'm a little rusty. Even if they agreed to let me play, and even if I read up on the rules again, talking during the game is frowned upon."

I also thought it would be a lot easier if there was something that both Jaxson and I could do together. I'm sure if I discussed it with him, he could come up with something. "I'll figure it out. The key here is that I would need to cut down on my hours waitressing when needed."

"Of course. I always knew this waitressing job wasn't a career for you."

I thought it was, despite knowing deep in my heart that I had more potential. "Thank you for understanding."

"Of course, dear. I want what is best for you—and Iggy,

of course. What did your parents say? I bet they were excited."

Since they always wanted me to have a career, I'm sure they would be. "I haven't mentioned it yet, but I will. I need time to think."

"No rush."

After we finished talking about my problems, I wanted to find out about Aunt Fern's upcoming hot date. "Have you seen Bob lately?"

"No, he called yesterday, but he said he was busy at work."

"Two more days until the big event!"

"Don't hold your breath. I'm having second thoughts. He's no Harold."

My heart ached for her. "I know, but he doesn't have to be. Think of him as a new adventure. Go out with him and have a good time. If it doesn't work out, all you've gained is—"

"A few pounds?" Aunt Fern laughed. "Yes, that is good advice. If I recall, I've given it to you a few times."

I smiled. "So you have."

She stood. "I need to get back downstairs. Good luck with your decision."

"Thanks."

When she left, I sank back against the sofa, needing to figure out the next step in my life. Even though Iggy tried to convince me to be an amateur sleuth, all I saw were hurdles.

What if I failed? What if no one ever asked for my help again?

Going for a walk might help clear my head. As I stood, someone knocked on my door. The strength of it implied a man. Only a dreamer would think it was Steve Rocker coming to ask me to help solve a case he couldn't.

The knock sounded again. "Glinda? It's Jaxson."

I blew out a breath. He was here to convince me to do this crazy adventure. "Coming."

When I opened the door, he rushed in carrying a laptop. "I know what will convince you to join forces with me."

This I had to see. "What is it?"

He turned around and grinned. "I made a spreadsheet with all of the pros and cons."

At that moment, I knew we'd be perfect partners.

Glinda's special Cranberry Sauce
[kind of looks like Cranberry Jelly]

Prep Time: 15 minutes.

Makes: about 1 1/2 cups

Ingredients

1 1/2 cup dried cranberries

3/4 cup cranberry juice

1/3 c. sugar

1/4 tsp salt

For the roux

2 TBL Cornstarch

4 TBL water to mix into the cornstarch to make the roux

Directions

1. Add all ingredients (except for the cornstarch and water) to a pot. Bring to a boil.

2. Reduce heat to a simmer until cranberries plump up. (Maybe 10 minutes). Add the cornstarch slurry slowly while stirring until it thickens.

3. Let it cool a bit and then place in a blender. Blend for 60 seconds.

4. Put in a small container and place a piece of parchment paper onto top to keep the skin from forming.

5. Put into refrigerator until ready to scoop it out!!

Glinda's special Yam Casserole

Makes six servings

Ingredients

A 29 oz can of Yams in heavy syrup

A 1-8 oz can of Pineapple-preferable crushed, but chunks are
okay if you are willing to dice them.

One small box of raisins

1/6 cup Sugar

1/4 cup Butter

1/4 cup Brown sugar

1/2 cup of small Marshmallows

Directions

1. Cut up the pineapple into small pieces with the knife
2. Put the butter in the pot and start melting on the stove
3. Open the can of sweet potatoes and strain away the juice #
4. Empty the sweet potatoes into the mixing bowl
5. Mash up the sweet potatoes with a fork
6. Pour the melted butter into the sweet potatoes and fold in
    with the fork
7. Add the sugar and brown sugar and fold in with the fork
8. Add the raisins and pineapple and mix with the mixer
9. Put it in the baking dish
10. Bake for 35 minutes at 350°
11. Put marshmallows on top just before serving

Enjoy!!

I hope you enjoyed seeing more of the townsfolk of Witch's Cove, and experiencing the life of her familiar, Iggy. Opening her own Pink Iguana Sleuth company with Jaxson Harrison brings a whole new dimension to her life.

Check out Sleuthing In The Pink (book 4 of A Witch's Cove Mystery.)

Don't forget to sign up for my Cozy Mystery newsletter *to learn about my discounts and upcoming releases. If you prefer to only receive notices regarding my releases, follow me on BookBub.*

http://smarturl.it/VellaDayNL
bookbub.com/authors/vella-day

Here is a chapter one of Sleuthing In The Pink.

"WHAT DO YOU think?" I held up the new wooden sign that my new partner in crime, Jaxson Harrison, promised he'd mount outside our new office tomorrow.

Penny Carsted, one of my best friends and fellow coworkers, raised her glass of wine in a toast. "It's amazing. To Glinda Goodall and The Pink Iguana Sleuths!"

I leaned the wooden plague against my sofa, grabbed my glass, and touched my drink to hers. "To the Pink Iguana Sleuths." I inhaled the joy, only to let reality seep in. I sighed.

"Is something wrong?" Penny asked.

Darn. I hadn't wanted to share my insecurities with her tonight, because she seemed so happy, but what were friends for?

"What if I'm making a mistake by starting my own firm—and with Jaxson, no less?" I slipped next to her on the sofa. "I mean, I'll be cutting down my hours significantly at the Tiki Hut. Not only will I miss talking and sharing things with you, the loss of income will put a serious dent in my savings."

"Since when have you ever worried about that kind of thing?" Penny asked.

"All the time?"

Penny took another sip of her wine. "That's nonsense. Staring your own firm is what the universe has always had in store for you. You're organized, focused, and determined to help others. Besides a few loss tips, it won't cost you much.

Didn't you say that Drake isn't charging you any rent for the office space?"

Drake was my best male friend who owned the two-story Howl at the Moon Wine and Cheese Emporium two buildings over from my second-floor apartment above the Tiki Hut Grill—make that my rent free apartment. I did have the best aunt in the world. He also was Jaxson's younger brother.

"Yes. I know it's perfect. Drake was using the second floor of his building as a storage room, but being the doll that he is, he straightened it up for me—more or less." I don't know why I was worried. "The best part is that our new office has an outside staircase, a small bathroom, and even a tiny kitchen—one that currently is stacked with empty wine boxes." As I said, the place was more or less cleaned up. "I'm pretty sure he would have charged me if his brother wasn't part of the deal."

Penny lifted a shoulder. "That could be, but since Drake wants his brother to be happy, he'll to do whatever it takes to make it happen. Besides, I think this new adventure will help both of you." She reached out and squeezed my hand.

"You're right."

Jaxson Harrison had come to town a few months ago after staying away from Witch's Cove for eleven years. Why that long? His hometown had accused him of a crime he hadn't committed. As a result, he'd served three years in jail for robbery. Thankfully, he was able to move forward with his life—kind of—by going back to school. Not only did he study some law, he earned a degree in computer science.

When he returned to test the waters, Witch's Cove was anything but friendly, thanks to the crooked sheriff and his deputy son. When the truth came out about out Jaxson's innocence—partially because of yours truly—his record was expunged. Ever since then Jaxson's outlook on life had improved greatly.

"I know I'm right," Penny said. "Now drink up."

I wanted to believe her worse than anything. "Jaxson told me that he was feeling a bit restless working in Drake's back room, but I hope he isn't just joining forces with me because I helped clear his name."

"Nonsense. I haven't spoken to him recently, but from what you've told me, he seems to like working on cases."

If anyone had told me a few months ago that I'd be partnering with Jaxson Harrison, I would have laughed in their faces. Not only hadn't he been my type when I was fifteen, Jaxson was even less my type when he returned home. He was angry. So angry.

After everyone learned that the sheriff had lied about Jaxson being the guilty party in the liquor store theft, his personality had totally transformed. It improved even more last week when the courts deemed Sheriff William Duncan— or rather Duncan Donut—guilty of lying on the stand. He received three years in jail, followed by three years probation, and a three thousand dollar fine. It wouldn't give Jaxson his time back, but it did help his mental state.

"I hope so, but the truth is, I worry about going into business with him," I said.

"I don't see why?" Penny finished off her glass of wine. "Jaxson seems great. And he treats you well."

"He does. For now. But what if he becomes too controlling? Being protective is one thing, but if he insists we do things his way, it might be a problem."

If we ended up fighting all the time, it could be a deal breaker, which was why I promised myself to avoid arguing at all costs.

"He won't do that. He knows you're the witch."

"A witch with few powers. Every spell I've done of late seems to mess up things even more."

Penny set down her glass and wrapped an arm around my shoulder. "Stop obsessing."

"Obsession is my middle name."

She laughed. "That is what will make you a successful professional sleuth."

"You think?"

She smiled. "I know so."

"Thanks." It helped having the support. My aunt was on board with this new adventure, but my parents? Not so much. They'd been hounding me forever to find a real job that would use my math degree, but being a sleuth was too dangerous in their minds. Oh, well. I couldn't please everyone. It was what I wanted, so it was what I was going to do.

Penny sat back up and refilled her glass with the bottle I'd left on the coffee table. When the two of us got going, we could plow through one in no time.

"I really love the name of your new company—and the pink signage."

Penny was clearly trying to change to subject to cheer me up, and I appreciated that. I chuckled. "Well, that is the only color I wear."

"And I'm pink," Iggy said, lifting his chest. He'd been sitting quietly—a rarity—on the edge of the coffee table for a while.

Iggy was my pink iguana familiar—make that my talking pink iguana. Anyone who hasn't been around Witch's Cove for long, might not know that when I was twelve, I went into the Hendrian Forest and conjured him up by doing a spell. Sure, I was hoping for a black cat—what twelve-year-old girl wouldn't wish for one—but I got Iggy instead. He claims he was born green, but when I came along, my obsession with wearing pink must have changed his color. Trust me, he hasn't let me forget it in the last fourteen years.

I will have to say that of late, he hasn't been complaining about it as much. It might be because I recently tried to do a spell to return him to his natural green state, but the spell went wrong—really wrong.

I inhaled to push aside my rather maudlin musings and smiled. I wanted Iggy to know how much I loved him. "Yes, everyone will flock to our company to ask for our help regarding their investigative needs, because I have the best pink iguana detective in Witch's Cove."

"I'm the only pink iguana in Witch's Cove or in all of Florida for that matter."

"True."

Poor Iggy. Ever since his new girlfriend refused to give him the time of day, he'd been a bit depressed. Then again, Aimee was a cat, so it was understandable.

"Is Jaxson okay with the firm's name?" Penny asked. "I thought he wanted Goodall and Harrison."

"He did at first, but the name wasn't exactly catchy. After we discussed it—and Iggy chimed in—Jaxson agreed with the new name mostly because he conceded that the firm is mine, and that he is still merely the muscle."

"I love it," Penny said. "And he is all muscle. I have to say, it takes a secure man to work at a company with that name."

"Jaxson is very sure of himself."

"Do you know what I think about the sign?" Iggy asked moving forward a bit, careful not to knock over the almost empty wine bottle.

I knew what he was going to say. "The best part is the pink iguana wearing the Sherlock Holmes' hat?" That and the name.

"Yup. And the magnifying glass implies I'm really smart."

I laughed. "You are smart, magnifying glass or not, but I thought it was a nice touch too. Putting your image on the sign was actually Jaxson's idea."

Having Jaxson Harrison as a partner—at least part time— was what convinced me to get into the amateur sleuth business in the first place. Would anyone actually pay us for our help? Only time would tell.

One thing for sure, if pursuing someone required me to carry a weapon, I'd have to turn the information over to Sheriff Rocker and let him handle it.

Our lawman was already aware that Iggy and I could communicate with one another, as well as the fact I was a witch with some abilities. It had taken work to convince him that the occult was real, but now that he was a believer, it would make providing my sources much easier. I no longer had to worry that he'd dismiss me, because I was some crazy waitress turned sleuth.

Buy SLEUTHING IN THE PINK

A WITCH'S COVE MYSTERY (Paranormal Cozy Mystery)
PINK Is The New Black (book 1)
A PINK Potion Gone Wrong (book 2)
The Mystery of the PINK Aura (book 3)
Sleuthing In The PINK (book 4)

HIDDEN REALMS OF SILVER LAKE (Paranormal
Romance)
Awakened By Flames (book 1)
Seduced By Flames (book 2)
Kissed By Flames (book 3)
Destiny In Flames (book 4)
Box Set (books 1-4)
Passionate Flames (book 5)
Ignited By Flames (book 6)
Touched By Flames (book 7)
Box Set (books 5-7)
Bound By Flames (book 8)
Fueled By Flames (book 9)
Scorched By Flames (book 10)

**FOUR SISTERS OF FATE: HIDDEN REALMS OF
SILVER LAKE** (Paranormal Romance)
Poppy (book 1)
Primrose (book 2)
Acacia (book 3)
Magnolia (book 4)
Box Set (books 1-4)
Jace (book 5)
Tanner (book 6)

WERES AND WITCHES OF SILVER LAKE (Paranormal Romance)
A Magical Shift (book 1)
Catching Her Bear (book 2)
Surge of Magic (book 3)
The Bear's Forbidden Wolf (book 4)
Her Reluctant Bear (book 5)
Freeing His Tiger (book 6)
Protecting His Wolf (book 7)
Waking His Bear (book 8)
Melting Her Wolf's Heart (book 9)
Her Wolf's Guarded Heart (book 10)
His Rogue Bear (book 11)
Box Set (books 1-4)
Box Set (books 5-8)
Reawakening Their Bears (book 12)

PACK WARS (Paranormal Romance)
Training Their Mate (book 1)
Claiming Their Mate (book 2)
Rescuing Their Virgin Mate (book 3)
Box Set (books 1-3)
Loving Their Vixen Mate (book 4)
Fighting For Their Mate (book 5)
Enticing Their Mate (book 6)
Box Set (books 1-4)
Complete Box Set (books 1-6)

HIDDEN HILLS SHIFTERS (Paranormal Romance)
An Unexpected Diversion (book 1)
Bare Instincts (book 2)
Shifting Destinies (book 3)
Embracing Fate (book 4)
Promises Unbroken (book 5)
Bare 'N Dirty (book 6)
Hidden Hills Shifters Complete Box Set (books 1-6)

MONTANA PROMISES (Full length contemporary
Romance)
Promises of Mercy (book 1)
Foundations For Three (book 2)
Montana Fire (book 3)
Montana Promises Box Set (books 1-3)
Hart To Hart (Book 4)
Burning Seduction (Book 5)
Montana Promises Complete Box Set (books 1-5)

ROCK HARD, MONTANA (contemporary romance
novellas)
Montana Desire (book 1)
Awakening Passions (book 2)

PLEDGED TO PROTECT (contemporary romantic
suspense)
From Panic To Passion (book 1)
From Danger To Desire (book 2)
From Terror To Temptation (book 3)
Pledged To Protect Box Set (books 1-3)

BURIED SERIES (contemporary romantic suspense)
Buried Alive (book 1)
Buried Secrets (book 2)
Buried Deep (book 3)
The Buried Series Complete Box Set (books 1-3)

A NASH MYSTERY (Contemporary Romance)
Sidearms and Silk(book 1)
Black Ops and Lingerie(book 2)
A Nash Mystery Box Set (books 1-2)

STARTER SETS (Romance)
Contemporary
Paranormal

Author Bio

Love it HOT and STEAMY? Sign up for my newsletter and receive MONTANA DESIRE for FREE. smarturl.it/o4cz93?IQid=MLite

OR Are you a fan of quirky PARANORMAL COZY MYSTERIES? Sign up for this newsletter. smarturl.it/CozyNL

Not only do I love to read, write, and dream, I'm an extrovert. I enjoy being around people and am always trying to understand what makes them tick. Not only must my romance books have a happily ever after, I need characters I can relate to. My men are wonderful, dynamic, smart, strong, and the best lovers in the world (of course).

My Paranormal Cozy Mysteries are where I let my imagination run wild with witches and a talking pink iguana who believes he's a real sleuth.

I believe I am the luckiest woman. I do what I love and I have a wonderful, supportive husband, who happens to be hot!

Fun facts about me

(1) I'm a math nerd who loves spreadsheets. Give me numbers and I'll find a pattern.

(2) I live on a Costa Rica beach!

(3) I also like to exercise. Yes, I know I'm odd.

I love hearing from readers either on FB or via email (hint, hint).

Social Media Sites

Website:
www.velladay.com

FB:
facebook.com/vella.day.90

Twitter:
@velladay4

Gmail:
velladayauthor@gmail.com

Made in the USA
Las Vegas, NV
08 July 2021

26102269R10116